Praise for

THE KISSING LIST

"Reents's characters are as sharp as they are sly, as intellectually brilliant as they are oddball. These stories are often funny, but there's a satisfying dark edge. . . . Reents weaves the book's stories together with humor, grief, and slender prose."

—*New York Times Book Review*

"The stories in *The Kissing List* are alternately ferocious, light-footed, sharp, and mordant; Stephanie Reents, in her first collection, proves herself to be a writer of terrific grace and power."

—Lauren Groff, author of the *New York Times* bestseller *The Monsters of Templeton* and *Arcadia*

"[An] invigorating debut. . . . Reents's witty narratives highlight the nuances of her characters' desires and hesitations."

—*Booklist*

"Stephanie Reents's stories are lucid, exciting, and unlike anything I've read before."

—Stephen Elliott, author of *The Adderall Diaries*

"Reents impresses with her knowledge of conflicted young-adult hearts and her astute portrait of their social lives. . . . Sharp work from a promising wri

Kirkus Reviews

"Formally adept . . . Reents has created a collection that is emotionally vivid and stylistically interesting."

—*Publishers Weekly*

"Gird yourself for the talent of Stephanie Reents, whose astringent wit and innovative, crunk-like rhythms could carry this collection alone."

—Leah Hager Cohen, author of *The Grief of Others*

"With sassy sexiness, sophisticated humor, and consummate intelligence, Reents draws us into her exploration of what it means to love . . . it's as compulsively readable as it is perceptive."

—Aurelie Sheehan, author of *History Lesson for Girls*

"*The Kissing List* is that rare phenomenon, a book that does justice to the complexity and ambivalence and hilarity of human relationships. . . . A moving and razor-sharp debut."

—Suzanne Rivecca, author of *Death Is Not an Option*

"Nothing you've read before will prepare you for these sly, funny, beautifully off-kilter stories. In Reents's hands, tragedy and comedy aren't so much related as indistinguishable, and the only happy marriage is between romance and despair. I guarantee *The Kissing List* will occupy a place in your heart."

—Eric Puchner, author of *Model Home*

THE KISSING LIST

THE KISSING LIST

Stories

Stephanie Reents

HOGARTH
London New York

This is a work of fiction. Names, characters, places, and incidents either are the product of the author's imagination or are used fictitiously. Any resemblance to actual persons, living or dead, events, or locales is entirely coincidental.

Published in the United States by Hogarth Paperbacks, an imprint of the Crown Publishing Group, a division of Random House, Inc., New York.
www.crownpublishing.com

HOGARTH is a trademark of the Random House Group Limited, and the H colophon is a trademark of Random House, Inc.

Originally published in hardcover in the United States by Hogarth, an imprint of the Crown Publishing Group, a division of Random House, Inc., New York, in 2012.

Library of Congress Cataloging-in-Publication Data
Reents, Stephanie, 1970–
The kissing list / Stephanie Reents.
p. cm.
1. Young women—Fiction. 2. Generation Y—Fiction.
3. New York (N.Y.)—Fiction. 4. Chick lit. I. Title.
PS3618.E437K57 2012
813'.6—dc23 2011038354

Grateful acknowledgment is made to the following for permission to reprint previously published material: New Directions Publishing Corp.: Excerpt from "This Is Just to Say" from *The Collected Poems: Volume 1, 1909–1939* by William Carlos Williams, copyright © 1938 by New Directions Publishing Corp. Reprinted by permission of New Directions Publishing Corp.

Carcanet Press Limited: Excerpt from "This Is Just to Say" from *The Collected Poems: Volume 1, 1909–1939* by William Carlos Williams. Reprinted by permission of Carcanet Press Limited.

Selected stories in this work were previously published in the following: *Epoch* magazine: "Disquisition on Tears" and "Roommates"; *Gulf Coast:* "Love for Women"; *New South:* "Little Porn Story."
"Disquisition on Tears" subsequently published in *O. Henry Prize Stories 2006: The Best Stories of the Year*, copyright © 2006 by Vintage Anchor Publishing, a division of Random House, Inc. (New York: Anchor Books, 2006).

ISBN 978-0-307-95183-0
eISBN 978-0-307-95184-7

Printed in the United States of America

BOOK DESIGN BY BARBARA STURMAN
COVER DESIGN BY CHRISTOPHER BRAND

10 9 8 7 6 5 4 3 2 1

First Paperback Edition

In memory of my grandmothers,

Jean Reents and Frances Bartron

Contents

KISSING

During that year, the year after the kissing list, I kissed a lot of people on the lips, unrelated to the usual factors such as gender, familiarity, or even sexual attraction. I traded spit on the corner of Houston and Mott with my out-of-town friend Dale, even though he was several inches shorter than me. I accidentally planted one on my college roommate and my best friend and running partner, Frances, too.

"You can't kiss me there," Frances said, playfully socking my bicep. "With this rock, I could mess you up." She pumped her fist, the almond-size diamond that she'd recently received glittering grotesquely. Then she gave me a quick, flirtatious lip brush back. "Don't tell my financier."

I smooched a coworker in the middle of his going-away party. We'd never exchanged more than two sentences, but that afternoon, I discovered his well-moisturized lips tasted of chocolate. I got mouthy with a man named Peter, who would later become my boyfriend. He teased me relentlessly about not inviting him up that night, but it was past the witching hour, and I knew our kissing would be merely a prelude to more serious activities. I kissed countless other people, people I've forgotten now, they were so insignificant. The only people I didn't kiss were those I actually wanted to: Lance and Laurie. But I'd lost Lance after that weekend in Santa Fe, and Laurie's immune system was so delicate I donned a surgical mask whenever I visited. Sometimes kissing doesn't count. Sometimes it does. Sometimes it's hard to tell the difference.

Take what happened with Anna. She and I had narrowly avoided a friend breakup during our graduate school days at Oxford over a certain incident in which Anna had kissed someone I was kissing and more than kissing, and I had kissed someone who was kissing (and perhaps more than kissing) someone else. Back then, Anna, Dixon, Vita, and I regularly got wasted at parties, standing underneath gloomy portraits of British aristocrats and drinking three-quid bottles of Portuguese wine. Vita, whom we called the tagalong, was a junior-year-abroader who lived in my house and sweetened our friendship with homemade pies. Dixon was my boyfriend and kissing partner, a black-haired, blue-eyed southerner whose greatest passions were arguing, college football, and antique marbles. And Anna, she was the voice of reason when Dixon got under my skin.

One evening, as we weave-walked home through the streets, I saw Dixon and Anna exchange a sideways glance and knew, as one only can after too much to drink, that there was something in the way they avoided each other's eyes.

"Are you . . . ?" I asked.

"What?" Vita giggled. "Yes, I freely admit it. I'm drunk." She started doing jumping jacks in the street.

"I'm not talking to you." I squared myself toward Dixon and Anna, but before I could ask my question, Anna opened her mouth, shook her head, clamped her mouth shut again, then spun around and zigzagged away down the sidewalk.

"Come on, Sylvie," Dixon said. "I'm sorry, but I swear it was just a stupid dare. We missed the bus back from London and shacked up in a hotel for the night. We were so drunk though . . ."

For effect he said, "It wasn't nothing, nothing at all. Just some fumbling and kissing."

He tried to put his arm around me, which would have been a victory at another time, but I fled, leaving him standing in front of a window full of chocolate shortbread and caramel-covered oatmeal bars. I ducked into the gardens of New College, stumbled through the rosebushes, and collapsed against a brick wall that had been built in the Middle Ages to fortress the town against marauding Luddites.

"Sylvie?" Vita's voice found me from across the quad.

"Go away!" I shouted back.

I watched in horror as a dark figure sprinted across the perfectly manicured lawn.

"Vita, stop."

Now she was next to me, petting my back: "Oh, Sylvie, Sylvie, Sylvie, poor Sylvie."

I shrugged her away. "Go home, Vita. You could get sent down for walking on the grass."

"But this is an emergency," she wailed.

"No," I said, "it's just a stupid thing." I dug a ten-pound note out of my pocket. "Now go to the High Street and get a cab."

"I can't leave you," she sniffled.

"You can," I said, unwrapping her arm from my shoulder. She wore a green tweed jacket that was big enough for two of her and a silly college scarf that she'd splurged on. She favored words like *splurge* and called this outfit her "intellectual getup," which was why, among other reasons, I felt protective of her. "I'll get you a cab," I said, pulling her to her feet and linking my arm through hers to keep her moving in a straight line.

A kiss is a kiss is a kiss is a kiss. Gertrude Stein claimed she reinvented the rose through repetition. I thought about how kisses burgeoned, blossomed—dry lip pecks into moist tangled tongues, repetition into habit. A kiss is a kiss is a kiss is a kiss. But a kiss was never just a kiss, even when it didn't convey affection. It wasn't that I loved Dixon; in fact, I despised him in a way that made his unfaithfulness more painful because he gained power in our already lopsided relationship. Dixon could argue anything, including the mutually exclusive positions that, on the one hand, fidelity signified nothing about your true affection for another person, and on the other, I should want him and no one else. When I tried to point out that his argument was a bunch of shit, he assaulted me with paragraph-long explanations and tender nuzzles. I don't want to admit it, but when Dixon wanted to kiss persuasively, wow!

I didn't love Anna either, but she was the closest thing I had to a best friend, the person who liked big Indian meals and running the muddy river paths, who was wicked smart but modest and shared my skepticism about the other Americans on our fellowship, most notably the Harvard grads who complained about being in exile and a small clutch of ironic men who turned themselves into zombies by refusing to budge from East Coast time. As the wind blew, damping out the moon like sand thrown on a fire, I hiccupped and wiped my nose across the sleeve of my black jacket. It was getting late, and I needed comfort or at least another drink.

Todd was at Maureen's. He was a friend, and Maureen was an intimidating enigma. She lived in a fourth-floor turret with a fireplace that she kept stoked with stolen books; her dissertation was on the antivivisection movement, and to support the cause, she shoplifted cookbooks with glossy pictures of mouthwatering steaks and rich, oily stew. "Cows, not cuts" was her motto. She favored short dresses, patterned tights, vegan boots, and bright red lipstick. I knocked on the door.

"Sylvie." Todd tucked a strand of honeyed hair behind his ear, looking happy to see me. His shoulder-length locks also fed my affection. "What's up?"

"Hey," Maureen said, drawing out the word.

They were both tipsy, but in those days we were always under the influence of something.

"Is monogamy old-fashioned?" I asked. "Does it count when you're drunk?"

"Bastard," Todd said, bandaging me in his arms. From the beginning, he'd opposed my dalliance with Dixon, but I wasn't sure whether it was because he liked me, or whether it was just an alpha-male kind of thing. He kissed me, and without thinking, I kissed him back.

"Sparks are flying." Maureen tossed a book on the fire. "I don't like this."

"Is he your boyfriend?" I said, suddenly mortified.

"Not technically." She forced a smile to her face. "Whatever."

"You said you couldn't seriously date a carnivore," Todd told Maureen. "How was I supposed to interpret that?"

The rhythm was less than satisfying: kiss, talk, kiss, talk.

"We should stop," I said, though my lips contradicted my words.

Maureen suddenly leapt from the bed and kissed us both on the cheek. She reeked of gin and lime. "My blessing."

Todd's lips got dry. "Really?"

"Be free. Like animals," she added.

"Really?" Todd repeated.

She exhaled wearily. I knew I was doing something I shouldn't, but I couldn't stop myself. Kiss, kiss. Kiss, kiss. It was like a reflex. Todd kissed me, and I kissed back. Maureen was standing on her tiptoes next to us, and we were standing in front of the fire, and I kissed Maureen once or twice, as did Todd, and she returned our kisses before screaming, "Enough!"

Todd and I went back to my house on a road lined with cheap Indian takeaways and kept kissing, just kissing, reposing but fully clothed, groping fruitlessly and frantically through fabric.

"We should have done this sooner," he gasped.

Instead of saying anything, I stamped his Adam's apple with my lips. Our tongues kept moving, making vaguely unpleasant slurpy sounds until we both passed out from frustration or fatigue or our earlier revelry, which had reduced us to little more than bodies.

The next morning, the sound of scratching woke me. Vita was pacing the hallway in flannel pajamas, her eyes moated. She pointed at the front door. "The enemy has made an appearance."

I couldn't help but smile at her flair for the dramatic. "My tutor?"

"No," she said. "Your betrayer. Shall I tell her to scram?"

"Why don't you make some coffee?" I said. "That would be useful."

I found Anna stretching her calves in the front concrete garden. Her cheeks were flushed, her hair pulled back into a high, tight ponytail. Her bare legs were bright red. I hopped from one foot to the other to keep my feet from freezing.

"You're still dressed?" she asked.

"Early morning run?" I said.

"Penance," she answered. "Up to the top of Cowley Road five times. Listen, Sylvie, I'm sorry. Dixon and I . . ." She scraped her teeth across her bottom lip. "We were really drunk, and we kissed, but nothing else happened."

It was still early enough in the morning that the clouds hadn't swept in and blotted out the sun. England sucked. I squinted at her. I wanted to slam the door in her face, but she was already on the verge of crying. "Have a great run."

Inside, Vita sat on the staircase, hugging her knees to her chest. She held up a mug of coffee hopefully. "Oh, Sylvie, are you okay?"

"No, and now I'm going back to bed."

Todd stirred after I crawled into our cozy tent of sheets. "When is a kiss just a kiss?" I pecked at his cheek as though my life depended on it.

"Hmm," he said. "That wasn't." And then we were starting all over again, our tongues bumping, our teeth trying to stay out of the way. I nibbled on his lip before giving him my best butterfly, the kind of kiss that was capable of arousing even a cold, depressed bastard like Dixon, and I hoped we'd carry on. That's all I wanted. Just a kiss.

After Anna allegedly "just kissed" Dixon, or Dixon allegedly "just kissed" Anna—the causality was never clear to me—I started a campaign to avoid Dixon. Vita volunteered to screen my calls, and from my bedroom or the kitchen, I often heard her lower her naturally high, sweet voice and growl, "She's not home," "Well, you should have thought of that earlier," and "Take some responsibility." When I actually saw Dixon scuttling around in his dirty gray windbreaker, I looked through him. I forgave Anna, or perhaps I just wanted to torture her, because once a week, we had lunch of ciabatta and hummus in her room overlooking the High Street, and Anna complained about the dart player she was kissing, who had strong wrists but weak lips, and I confessed Todd's technique could stand some improvement (his mouth was often pressed into a grimace), or I cried over Dixon, who had hardly ever kissed me because he was too depressed, but had willingly kissed her, and Anna looked stricken and asked me about Maureen, who had lost Todd in the name of comforting me. These lunches were painful.

I spent more time with Todd, who kissed away my worries and took me to literary festivals. Like the poor on pilgrimages, we bussed around England (the thought of our slobbery PDAs makes me shudder now) seeking transcendental moments: alone in the loo with James Fenton, sharing a cigarette with William Trevor, et cetera, et cetera. Once, through sheer persistence, we swung an invitation to dinner with Seamus Heaney, along with a whole party of minor writers, parasitic worshippers (us), rising stars, and falling-down drunks. Todd sat next to our idol, while I ended up next to an Irish poet named Maeve C.

"His lips look like an eel's vagina," she said, nodding at Seamus Heaney.

I didn't want to talk to Maeve but had no choice since the man on my left spoke a language that didn't sound like English, even though it was.

"Have you heard of female condoms?" she asked, spewing small pieces of iceberg lettuce and cucumbers. "They're all over Belfast."

"Really," I said.

"The women are walking around with latex fluttering out of their weenies." She giggled.

I tried to catch Todd's eye, but he was having a moment with Seamus, not quite talking to him, but nodding his head enthusiastically in response to something that a poet on Seamus's other side was saying.

"You're in love with him too," Maeve whispered, so close her warm breath moistened my neck.

Everything from the crumbed and fried cod to the pale potatoes on our plates was as anemic as the winter sun. I felt vaguely sick.

I had been kissing (and more than kissing) Todd for six weeks, but it was all motion and mechanics, our passion reserved for long discussions about contemporary British poetry. I tried to pretend he really wanted me (we were kissing, after all), but on some level, I knew he still wanted Maureen just as I still wanted Dixon, even though he'd once made fun of the way I kissed, accusing me of leading too aggressively with my tongue, just as Dixon still wanted everyone because it was fun to get drunk, and the electricity right before you kissed, when you didn't know whether your tongues would touch or not, was amazing. First kisses were always thrilling, even if you were depressed, or perhaps especially if you were depressed. Vita wasn't kissing anyone. She was scandalized—that's the word she used—after she'd needled me into admitting that Todd had been in my bed that morning. "How could you," she cried, "when you'd just had your heart broken by Dixon?" She believed in a better version of me than I did. I didn't dare tell her about Maureen.

I couldn't stop crying. I attributed the abundance of my emotions to the gray winter or my overidentification with Margery Kempe, a woman I was reading for my thesis on female mystics, who wandered around the British Isles during the Middle Ages, bursting into tears every time she thought about Christ's sacrifice. I didn't want to accept the possibility that I was crying over a stupid kiss—misdirected, alcohol induced, hard lipped, empty. I know it's trite, but so much of what is crippling is. Cuckoldry is cuckoldry is cuckoldry is cuckoldry is cuckoldry is cuckoldry is cuckoldry is cuckoldry. With enough repetition, it starts to sound like *cuddly,* the word made new. I wish it was that easy.

The table erupted in laughter. I sniffled.

"What's wrong?" Maeve swept back her tangle of brown hair, and three bobby pins tinkled onto her place mat.

"Cuckoldry" was all I could think to say.

"Give me your hand." She studied my palm as if reading a map. "A very good hand."

I wanted her to say more, but the dinner party was breaking up. Todd caught my eye and flicked up his thumb like the blade of a knife. He must have had a word with the poet. As I was going out into the night, the air as clammy as a damp sponge, someone tugged my sleeve. Maeve held out a wine-glass. "The lips of Seamus Heaney touched this glass." She smiled, and her face crumpled like a paper bag. Being a poet was hard work.

"Take it," she said. "It's as close as you'll come to kissing him."

I never kissed Seamus Heaney, though I did kiss (and more than kiss) Dixon again after Todd and I finished kissing and he went back to Maureen. Dixon was initially repentant, eager and accepting of my kisses, but a one-month stretch of snogging along the damp banks of the Thames gave me a head cold, plus Dixon was too depressed to share a bed. When Vita found out about our afternoon quickies (all Dixon had the energy for), she was so furious she started haunting our house, leaving notes instead of speaking to me. Once, after copious amounts of red wine, I tried to explain the invisible but potent aphrodisiac qualities of Dixon's intelligence, but she just gave me a withering look and said: "Get real, Sylvie. You're not fucking the guy's mind."

"Good point," I said.

Dixon and I broke up and got together three more times before we finally went our separate ways.

The funny thing about being in your early twenties is that it's a lot like being any other age, except you don't know it.

For a long time, you think you'll change and become a better version of yourself, but really, you just wind up being a little more tolerant of the person you've always been. Or something like that. That year when I thought I should be more mature, I kept kissing people—on the lips, on the cheek, sometimes on the chest and other not readily accessible places. I kissed friends, I kissed strangers, I kissed people I had no intention of kissing, had never dreamed of kissing. I made out with an usher at Todd's wedding. Maureen was there, her lipstick a slightly more subdued shade of fuck-you red. She sniffed the mini-quiches in her napkinned hand. "I eat animal by-products now," she said, "but crusts are dangereux."

As Todd fed his bride, a lawyer named Rhadika, a nibble of cake and then kissed her—long, long, long—I didn't feel the stirring of anything, or at least not much. Right then, I wished Vita might magically appear in a funky dress she'd thrifted and her grandma's rhinestones, take me aside, and whisper about how it was weird to see an old flame do it. "Poor Sylvie," she'd say "Not that Todd was the one, but it still feels icky." I could protest that it was no big deal, maybe convincing myself in the process that it wasn't. I'd lost track of Vita after she graduated. It made me sad. If she'd been there, I probably would have kissed her, too.

Just then, the DJ called all the single ladies to the dance floor for the bouquet toss, and in that brief lull of scraping chairs and quiet groans and damp-palmed excitement, someone yelled, "Not me," and I turned to see Maureen careen out of the room.

The usher said, "That girl is a piece of work."

I smiled at him. Kissing was easier than talking, and the usher kissed fairly well, loose lipped, not too wet. We exchanged e-mail addresses, but I knew we wouldn't stay in touch, even though he was tall and handsome, a guy's guy whose family had made its fortune in trailer parks. Later that night, I stood in front of the bathroom mirror, in the apartment I shared with two nice men who were always offering to set me up with their nice eligible friends, and asked myself: "Is this one for the couch or the cosmetics counter, darling? Do you need your head shrunk or your face scrubbed? Electroshock or electrolysis?"

The evening when I thought this spell finally broke was much like the evening when Dixon kissed Anna or Anna kissed Dixon (and who knew what else!), the evening I kissed Todd and Maureen kissed us both, offering a blessing she regretted the next day. That is to say, Anna and I were drunk.

By now, though, we had grown up enough that it only required three beers to make us silly. "If it still matters to you, I think we should talk about it," she said gravely, bringing up the ancient history that drew us into permanent intimacy.

I watched her fiddle with her pearls. That was one of the things that had irked me at the time, the fact that Dixon had kissed someone who wore pearls, but I now half-wished that I was the kind of woman who could pull them off. They gave Anna a certain sheen. I slid my nail under the label of my bottle of beer, considering what I wanted to say. Anna leaned toward me.

"You weren't there. Let me explain what happened."

I had a moment to decide whether I wanted to hear or not, whether I wanted to find out who kissed who, or who kissed whom. Would the truth set me free? I giggled at the thought.

Anna was leaning in, and I leaned in—maybe I was on the verge of whispering, "Yeah, tell me what happened," but instead my lips found hers. This way, that way, and then this way again. It felt dangerous and familiar. A murmur of conversation drifted downstairs as the host and her friend got ready for bed, and Anna's eyes rose, lines etching her forehead. I could tell she was considering the likelihood of someone appearing at the top of the staircase and catching us, but I didn't care.

"Am I scandalizing you?" I asked, before pulling her back to me. This delighted me, the thought of unnerving Anna, of derailing a conversation that she'd surely control if we used our lips and tongues for making words. Her mind was just as sexy as Dixon's, and she was much, much nicer. She kissed me back, and we kept kissing, pressed together on another woman's sofa, and after a long while, during a brief flash of drunken clarity, when I asked whether she was freaked out, hoping I might freak her out simply by asking, she laughed and said, "Oh, Sylvie, you of all people should know better. It's just kissing." Then she gave me mouth to mouth one last fierce and tingly time, and though I'd like to say this brought me back to life, it only woke me up enough to follow Anna to the door, where she sent me on my way.

ROOMMATES

Of the things that I remember, one of them is the size of the apartment. It was so small that my roommate, Laurie, usually kept the Styrofoam head on the blond-wood kitchen table, its smooth face turned toward the mirrored bathroom door about five feet away, as if it were primping. When I would come home late at night, the head would greet me, wearing its regal copper-colored wig. At work, whenever my mind wandered from whatever manuscript I was proofreading, I would think about the head, bald during the day, turning away from the mirror and surveying our apartment, looking dubiously at the shabby blue couch against the window, the matching armchair, lumpy with springs, the front door with its collage of locks, the kitchen, or what there was of a kitchen in the shoebox-size fifth-floor walk-up that we shared. The Styrofoam head couldn't see, but I daydreamed that it sensed how things were.

Just before I moved in with Laurie, I had ditched my job as a reporter at a small-town newspaper and hopped on a transcontinental train with two duffel bags and $1,500 from the sale of my already secondhand Subaru. Taking the train seemed like a romantic way to start fresh in New York. Unfortunately, it was really just the kind of idea that sounded wonderful to say to other people. The train lost power for five hours outside of Denver and again right before St. Louis, and though I'd imagined the other passengers would be people like me, people embarking on life-changing adventures, they were mostly retirees and families with overtired children. I didn't blame the children for running through the cars. I felt just as restless. By the time the train pulled into Penn Station, I had covered dozens of index cards in intricate geometric patterns. It was as if I had spent the whole journey squinting into a kaleidoscope at bits of colored plastic and had never gazed out the window and seen cows moving across fields, or friends and lovers waiting at stations, or darkness slowly snuffing out the world.

Laurie was the sorority sister of a friend of mine from Oxford. I didn't know many sorority sisters, so this alone made me nervous about whether we'd be compatible. Laurie's roommate, a social worker, had moved out to the suburbs to save money. Laurie was thinking about offering the room to a homeless woman named Zahara who lived in front of the nearby Banana Republic, but instead she decided to take me as her roommate. The day I moved in, it snowed. It took me two trips by subway to bring my stuff from Brooklyn, where I had been camping out in a studio a friend was house-sitting. On the walk back and forth from the subway, I smoked cigarettes, the third pack I'd ever bought. Smoking outside in the cold didn't look that different from breathing. Between the two trips, I ordered a futon for delivery. Laurie had left a plastic juice pitcher of flowers in my new room. They were nothing fancy, just a bouquet of deli daisies and green filler, but they made me feel welcome.

Several days later, there were more flowers, except this time the whole apartment was filled with long-stemmed roses. Every surface, even the back of the toilet, held a jar or vase, and the scent was so powerful, you could smell it from the stairwell.

"My ex feels bad," she said.

I was expecting the usual story about how he'd cheated on her and was trying to win her back. I'd seen that before. Instead, Laurie gathered a handful of her hair and lifted it from her head. "The Frankenstein scar," she said, briefly explaining how nine months before, her cancer had reoccurred, and another tumor above her left ear had been removed. The scar looked like a miniature railroad track. "That damn intern shaved more than he had to. You should have heard the doctor cuss him out," she said. "He was pretty cute, though. No ring."

I think I said, "Oh, Laurie, that's terrible," or something else equally meaningless. I'm sure I teared up. My friends teased me that I'd cry if a friend of a friend of a friend hit a squirrel, and what's worse, I'd be blubbering for the squirrel, too.

But her cancer was terrible. And there was also something terribly audacious about flirting with the intern just before he cut into your skull. Maybe I laughed because I could tell she wanted me to, because I knew she needed someone else to share the dark humor of the situation. The task of remembering is so difficult sometimes.

"Let's hope the cancer is finito," she said before changing the subject. "What's your deal? Are you looking for love?" The way she said it made me laugh.

I was involved in a platonic affair with a sports doctor named Lance. He'd actually been my doctor back home when I was a teenager and fractures spun across my legs like cobwebs from running too many miles. We weren't friends until my senior year, when I'd booked an appointment with him to look at my knee, a casualty of college competition. I can't remember how, but the subject of dinner came up. When I met him at a nice restaurant later in the week, he was reading a book on female sexuality in Caribbean literature. Because I was so much younger than him, I found his interest in this subject sweetly hokey.

After I finished at Oxford and moved back west, he started sending me tickets to join him in different places. We met in Denver for a Sheryl Crow concert. We met in San Francisco and rode across the Golden Gate Bridge on rented bikes. We went to places where neither of us lived and dined at expensive restaurants. We weren't having a relationship. He had frequent-flier miles out the wazoo, and he felt sorry for me, stuck in a small town in western Wyoming, even though that's where I thought I wanted to be. "From Merry Old England to an armpit," he'd say, not entirely kindly. We talked a lot, but never about anything that had happened the week before. I didn't even know whether he had a girlfriend. At the end of the night, when I was tucked into a separate bed or bedroom—in New Orleans, I slept on sofa cushions on the floor—I imagined being his real girlfriend. I listened for him to slip out of his bed. I waited for him to lie down next to me. Since he was older, I thought he should make the first move. When I decided to try my luck in New York, he bought my cross-country train ticket. I was both grateful and confused, since it meant we'd be farther apart.

When Laurie and I were in the apartment at the same time, we usually sat across from each other at the table, since both the couch and the armchair were uncomfortable and our bedrooms were only big enough for beds. Sometimes we'd play chess. She always beat me. Concentrating on the black and white pieces made me feel tired.

"Your turn," Laurie said one night after we'd already played two games. She said chess was good exercise for her. "Oops. Are you sure you want to do that? Your queen is going to be vulnerable."

I moved my pawn and took a bite from the slice of pizza that I'd bought from the stand across the street. This, along with hothouse tomato and iceberg salads, was just about all I ate. Laurie took a sip of Diet Coke. Besides my meager salad makings and milk, the only other things the refrigerator contained were one or two of her half-drained Coke bottles.

"How's the job?" she asked.

"It's tough," I answered. "I'm beginning to think my boss is psycho."

"Why?"

"She threw a box of Kleenex at me today."

"You're kidding." She moved her rook. "That's really fucked up. Sounds like you should get a new job."

"I know."

"There's always demand in publishing."

"Not really," I said.

"With your résumé, you shouldn't have any problems."

Her next move put me in checkmate.

"You're right," I said, though all I could think of were millions of reasons I couldn't get a new job, especially since I'd only had my current one for three months.

"How's el doctor?" Laurie said as she gathered all the pieces, the black ones first, even though they'd end up jumbled together in her wooden box. "When's your next rendezvous?"

I watched as she stood on her tiptoes to bring the Styrofoam head down from the top of the refrigerator. It had been next to a box of cornflakes, also part of my limited diet. The reason I didn't cook was because I didn't think Laurie owned any pots or pans. Months later when I finally found them in the oven, where Laurie's old roommate had stowed them, it was because I'd decided to get creative and make myself a baked potato.

"Nothing planned." I tried to sound casual, even though I found myself rehearsing imaginary conversations with Lance where I'd confess I had a major crush on him, and he'd admit he felt the same about me.

Without even turning and looking in the mirror, she lifted the wig off her own head and slid it onto the fake one. "I don't get it. Do you get it?" she asked, licking her fingers.

She spun the head so that it was gazing at me. "No," the featureless face said. "He takes you places, but then nothing happens."

"We're just friends," I protested. "He's a lot older than me. Maybe . . ." But I didn't have an explanation that made sense. I wasn't even sure of his age.

"I think he's playing with you," Laurie said, beginning to twirl sections of hair into tight spirals. Without the wig, she looked like a Brooklyn punk with Upper East Side eyebrows.

"Stop ganging up on me." I addressed the head. "Make Laurie play nice."

She swiveled it back, so that it was facing her again. Without the wig, the head had no front or back. "We're just worried is all," she said, and then in the mock girlie voice that she reserved for her Styrofoam sidekick: "El doctor would be crazy not to snap you up."

Laurie's ventriloquism unnerved me. I knew she was just

trying to be funny, but I was as skilled at playing this game as at putting her in checkmate. "You're so traditional, Miss Brain. Isn't it possible to be friends with men?" I immediately regretted the first part.

"Oh, Sylvie," she said, "don't be so naive. Guys are a different species. They don't think the way we do."

"As though we think alike," I said.

"Oh, how it pains you," she said, pretending to stab herself in the sternum, "a dagger through your heart."

"Shut up," I said, still leaning toward her.

"I am woman. Hear me roar." She howled.

I rolled my eyes. "Do you even know who said that?"

"Except for the fried ovaries, the male pattern hair loss," she continued. "Why couldn't I lose the hair on my legs and you know where?"

I found myself smiling.

"Think of the advertising potential," she continued. "Chemo: better than a bikini wax."

I grabbed the head. I'd never done this before. "We'll make millions," I said in the head's high voice. "We'll move into a penthouse."

In old photographs of Laurie, her hair is the color of amber, thick and straight. She has sparkly green eyes and freckles, which she almost always powdered over. She wore short skirts and high heels, even though she walked unsteadily once her balance began to falter. I envied her style. In the middle of a thunderstorm one night, the dusky restaurant guys from across the street called out, “Nice legs!” as she struggled to find her keys. They invited her for supper. She rang the bell and told me to come along. Despite the fact that the intercom garbled everything, I could hear the excitement in her voice. I changed into my going-out-on-the-town clothes and took the stairs two at a time.

Laurie didn’t meet Lance, because he never came to visit me in New York. Once, after coming home from a bar where a man had bought me a drink, I decided to call him. My plan was to tell him that I like *liked* him and find out how he felt. Why not? We e-mailed and sometimes even exchanged letters, but we rarely spoke over the phone. When he answered, my nerves filled my throat, turning my voice into something heavy and hard to move. “Hi,” I choked out, “it’s Sylvie.”

Lance brightened. “It’s good to hear from you.”

As we talked about small things, I felt somewhat calmer. Finally I broached the subject: “You should come to New York sometime.”

“Why would I want to do that?” he asked.

I could tell he was joking, and yet it was enough to blow out my little flame. “It’s a great city,” I said.

“It’s a pretty good city,” he said, “but it’s not L.A.”

And then we started to compare the merits of the two cities and playfully argue, and by the time we exchanged chaste good-byes ten minutes later, I realized that, as far as he and I were concerned, I was still lost: a red balloon drifting above gray buildings in a clip from a movie.

I didn't meet Laurie's ex until after we'd been living together for a year, and she had relapsed again. It wasn't a big deal, she insisted, and to prove her point she threw a big boozy party—her relapse bash—at a friend's spacious apartment on the Upper East Side. I was predisposed to loathe Bradley. Through Laurie, who had a standing date with him each week, I knew Bradley was dating someone new, a woman our age who wasn't sick. Laurie called her the bimbo because she was a secretary. Once Bradley finished fucking her—that's what Laurie said the rare times she felt sorry for herself—he'd come back to her.

"Sylvia," Bradley said, offering me his hand. "I've heard so much about you."

He was handsome in a buttoned-up, stick-up-your-ass kind of way.

"Really," I said, eyeing the cuffs rolled up to show off his thick forearms and heavy gold watch. All that was missing was a pinky ring. "I bet I've heard more about you."

He laughed, missing my obvious sarcasm.

"How is she?" he asked. "I mean, really?"

"She's fine." I took a big sip of my scotch and soda and nearly spit it out.

Bradley studied me expectantly.

"What more can I tell you? She's fine."

"I just feel so guilty, you know," he said touching my arm the way men do when they're trying to get something from you.

I drew back as though his hand was a straightening iron. I thought he was going to tell me the story that I knew from

Laurie: about how good he'd been to her, about the totally normal doubts after graduation—how they had to sow their oats and date other people and blah, blah, blah . . . And then Laurie relapsed.

I was nodding from habit.

"I just got engaged. I don't know how to tell her."

I saw Laurie out of the corner of my eye. She was laughing, and though I couldn't hear her over the music and loud stupid conversations that people were having because it was a party, after all, and they'd already forgotten the occasion, or because, like me, they were torn between believing the doctors would remove every last grain of cancer and it would never happen again and wondering about the odds of this, and drinking too much to forget, I knew she was letting loose. I knew her laughter was big and true, that it was coming from someplace deep inside of her that I longed to find in myself.

Bradley glanced over his shoulder to see what was more interesting than him. When he turned back, he looked like he was choking.

Fucking Bradley. I wanted to kick him in the shin or stomp on his polished loafers. I planned to whisper, "I will kill you if you tell her." But instead I found myself grabbing his shoulders and pressing myself against him. "I'm sorry," I whispered.

The second time Laurie relapsed, eight months later, she didn't have a party—many of her friends seemed to be away—so I proposed a private send-off at the Italian restaurant around the corner. It was an unseasonably warm May day;

people were out in their summer clothes, despite the fact that they were still pale. The restaurant was just past a baseball diamond with an asphalt surface where kids played Little League on the weekends and teenagers sped around on skates, hacking the cement with their sticks, during the week. We sat on a bench and started drinking our first bottle of Chianti as we waited for a table underneath the wide red awning. A woman passed and began screaming, "My ring, my ring!" She pointed into the metal grate in the sidewalk in front of us. "My engagement ring slipped off my finger!"

"Princess," Laurie commented. "You'd think she just dropped her baby into the sewer."

Someone decided that the fireman across the street might be able to solve the problem. Sure enough, he swaggered over, unlocked the grate as if he were opening a cellar door, and descended beneath the city. When he climbed back out, the ring was cupped in the palm of his hand.

"Did you see the size of it?" I said. "It could have been a baby."

The whole restaurant broke into applause.

By the time we sat down for dinner, Laurie and I were in the middle of an argument, a stupid argument about whether people aspired to be famous so that they could influence others, or whether fame was simply a by-product of doing things for their own sake.

"Everyone wants to be on the front page of the *Times*," Laurie said between bites of spaghetti carbonara. "Think of the high you'd get from knowing that millions of people are reading about you."

I wanted a cigarette. I never smoked in front of her, though sometimes I smoked in my room, balanced on the window ledge, hoping the running T-shirt stuffed in the crack underneath the door would absorb the smell. "I doubt Bill Gates really cares," I said.

"You can't tell me you wouldn't die to be on the front page of the *Times*."

"Above or below the fold?"

This time, Laurie rolled her eyes at me. The waiter came by and uncorked another bottle of wine and set it next to the vase of purple tulips.

Laurie said, "Ciao bello." Two tables away a man with slicked-back hair and a yellow tie thoughtfully sipped his wine. "Maybe we should invite him over."

"No," I answered.

"I could send him a note." She swept her hair over her shoulder. It always amazed me how natural it looked.

"I thought you were my date tonight."

We argued often, though I can hardly remember much of what we argued about. One of our disagreements—one that never really ended—was about whether one of my friends should take the uptown subway late at night to her neighborhood at the northern tip of Manhattan. I thought it was fine; she was a grown-up, after all, and she had chosen to live up there. Laurie thought we should chip in for her cab fare, and from there the whole matter swiftly turned into an argument about the risks involved in taking the subway through Harlem and all its nasty implications. I often regret how much I argued with Laurie, but I also remember how much she loved it. When we got going, she could really irritate me, and then the apartment would seem even smaller than it actually was, and I would hate the sitcoms she watched on TV, and having a TV, period. And I would hate the fact that she bought fingernail polish every week, always some shade of peach, and then left the bottles on the window ledge behind the couch. And hating all these things would make me feel small.

"You're no fun, Sylvie," she said. "All I want is a little nookie before another chunk of my brain comes out. How can you deny me that?"

She laughed. The waiter brought dessert wine and tiramisu. It was on the house, he declared, winking at her. Men were always winking at her.

"What a sweet thing to do," she purred.

"He's interested," I said.

She glanced at the waiter as he walked away. "Too short."

"Oh, I don't know," I said. "Short men are sexy." Beyond the cheerful, bright noisiness underneath the awning, it was dark. The traffic going north on Sixth streamed silently by as if the cars and cabs were far removed and the only thing that mattered was the two of us winding each other up.

By the end of the evening, we were so wasted that Laurie talked me into betting half a month's rent that she could kiss five men in less time than I could. We agreed to keep a running tally taped on the refrigerator. Some tongue had to be involved for the kiss to count. It seems absurd now that we made this bet right before she was going to have surgery, but I suspect she knew I'd need a head start.

When I finally saw Lance, Laurie had relapsed again.

"Third time's a charm," she told me before I left. "Lucky me. I go under the knife and then up into a cloud of chemo."

Lance was waiting for me at the Albuquerque airport. It was awkward at first since we didn't hug. This was how it always was. We didn't touch each other, though I thought about touching him and being touched by him. I tried to recall what it had felt like when he had been my doctor. I tried to imagine his fingers tracing the pain of the stress fractures on my left tibia, or his thumb pressing into the hollow of my right hip, where the iliotibial band finished its journey from the knee.

For some reason, I remember the strangest things, none of them important. For example, I don't remember the name of the park we passed through on the way to Santa Fe. We even stopped and went for a hot, dusty hike there. And I don't remember the town where we stayed the first night, which was somewhere near the park. Instead, I remember the way Lance pinched his tongue between his index finger and thumb to wet them before he turned each page in the New Mexico guidebook. I remember the metallic taste in my mouth after we had hiked for three hours without water.

Laurie was losing her short-term memory. The brain is so compact, so specific. She boasted that nothing embarrassed her anymore. Shame or humiliation, or whatever you want to call it, was only a half teaspoon of gray matter. Things you didn't expect were just cells.

I imagined I might tell Lance some of these details. He was a doctor, after all. We went to a spa in the hills above Santa Fe. The footpath from the parking lot was made from gray and brown river stones, so shiny it was as if they were still underwater. In the lobby, there was an elaborate fountain that looked like a waterfall but smelled fake. In separate dressing rooms, we removed our clothes and put on plaid summer-weight robes. A quiet man led us along another shiny stone path to a gate in a cedar fence. Inside, there was a small hot tub bubbling with the spa's renowned mineral water.

"This doesn't bother you?" he asked.

I lied. I said boisterously, "I'm the least modest person I know," hoping that I might believe it by saying it. I said so many things. I often said, for example, "It is hard, but we're just roommates. We just live together." Period. End of story.

Lance slid off his robe and eased his body into the water. That's a lie. I don't know the precise way he disrobed and entered the pool, though not because I don't remember, but because I didn't watch. It's so laughable now. I decided that everything would be okay if I didn't actually see him naked. I stared into the empty space above his right shoulder as we both got undressed. In the hot tub, I kept my eyes fixed to his face: his eyes were the color of blue marbles, his nose was crooked, and his thin, pink lips were always slightly parted. Because of an old basketball injury, he couldn't breathe through his nose. That was another thing I liked about him. He'd played Division I basketball. I let my eyes fall to his chest. His hair was graying around his face, and the hair on his chest was gray too. The thermometer tied to the edge of the pool read 103. I forced myself to stay submerged, even though I wanted to get out.

"How's New York?" he asked.

"It's good." I felt as though I was being hard-boiled.

"How's your roommate?" he asked.

"Well . . ." It was hard to put into words. "I think she's fine."

He pushed himself up one step and sat waist-deep.

"Her cancer's benign," I said, even though I knew that no tumor was harmless. All of them could potentially displace important brain functions, Laurie had explained to me, but hers wasn't that terrible. That's what she said. All things considered. She had been in remission for five years before she started relapsing. "She's very optimistic," I insisted. "The tumors are only Grade 2."

Lance's expression changed. "How many times has it reoccurred?"

"Three times in the last two years," I said.

"That's serious, Sylvia. There's a good chance she could die."

I ended up looking down. I didn't want to, because I was afraid of what I might see beneath the surface of the water. But I couldn't look at Lance's face. And I couldn't get out of the hot tub either.

When I came back from Santa Fe, I didn't have a name to add to the kissing list. Neither did Laurie, but she had a good excuse. I had no idea how it was all going to work, now that the doctors had decided it was time to try the more aggressive chemo. Laurie toted home a plastic shopping bag filled with glass vials and hypodermic needles. It's surprising how soft our bodies are, how easy it was to insert the tip of the needle into her thigh, how the flesh would yield. Still, I couldn't believe that the doctors expected her to give herself shots. I pulled the needle from its plastic package, taking care not to touch and contaminate it. I inserted it into the vial, drew the liquid out, and then flicked the needle to make the air bubbles rise and pop. An air bubble could kill her. I searched for a place on her thigh that wasn't already bruised and stuck in the needle, plunged the plunger, drew it out, watching her blood surface and bead. We sat on the uncomfortable, lumpy couch with the TV turned to shows with loud, fake laugh tracks. She took pills, too, and went to the hospital every three days, where she got more drugs through an IV.

Maybe, if I had seen Lance again during that time, I would have told him about all of this; I would have spilled my life like a glass of red wine, ruining the perfect white tablecloths at the restaurants where we ate. I thought about calling him, but I was too afraid. I couldn't tell anyone what it was like to be sharing a small apartment with a roommate—a woman my age, someone who sometimes irritated me so much that I wasn't as nice as I should have been—who was dying. What could he have said? "It's terrible." That's what I told myself when I drank so much that I felt myself dissipating into atoms and exhaled my thoughts as carelessly as I breathed.

That weekend in Santa Fe, we had stayed in a bed and breakfast in a tiny town with a cemetery south of the city. Our room had one bed, but there was a futon in the corner.

"Do you want me to sleep there?" Lance asked.

"Don't be silly," I said. "We can share."

In the middle of the night, I woke up, feeling someone else's heat, the hair on his chest against my back, his arm around my shoulders. I rolled away, did a double roll. His hand hit the bed. He whispered, "Come back, Sylvia. I want to be with you," but I could not let myself move toward him. I lay quietly, my arm hanging off the edge of the bed, my fingertips skimming the cool, wooden floor, thinking about Laurie. She was probably alone in her double bed, the only sounds in our tiny apartment the careless noise of the street and the hushed breathing of the head.

We lived in a fifth-floor walk-up. Perhaps I should have emphasized that earlier. All those steps from the entrance on Bleecker Street to the door to our apartment. Laurie paused on each landing to catch her breath. This could have been before she relapsed for a fourth time or after. The stairwell was always empty, until one day when it filled with the sweet smell of flesh, more pungent than the ripest cheese. It was so powerful that I would clothespin my nose between my two fingers and take the stairs by twos, and still I could smell the odor through my mouth. The woman in apartment 2D stayed in bed for at least a week, and then it was the smell that aroused suspicion, not her disappearance. She was old, and evidently no one noticed her absence.

The living go on remembering; that's our job, to the extent we can bear our own scrutiny. My nightly conversations with Laurie were the chorus of a song, the same thing, night after night as we sat playing chess or watching TV. We talked about my complicated love life. I couldn't tell her that Lance had finally made a move and I'd done nothing. We talked about Bradley and his bimbo, and I wondered whether she knew they were engaged. We talked about my terrible job. We talked about whether we should get a summer share. We argued about politics.

I told her I was moving out one morning as she stood in front of the mirror getting ready for work. The red wig fell to the middle of her back, curling at the tips. It was impractical, she said all the time, too long. She should get it cut. She was beautiful, though, whether she was wearing the wig or a scarf.

On the table, the Styrofoam head eyed me suspiciously.

"When do you want to move?" she asked.

"Not immediately," I said. "In a month or two."

The list was still on the refrigerator, though there was nothing written under either of our names. I saw her expression change in the mirror. Her mouth opened, closed, then she smiled and laughed.

She said, "Okay," or that's what I try to remember, along with the talking Styrofoam head, the kissing list, the silly arguments, her expert opening moves, all the bottles of Diet Coke and fingernail polish, the lilt in her voice, the waiter calling out across the street to her: "Nice legs." This and everything else are what I try to think about, not the night several months later when she ripped the IV tubes from her arm and descended by elevator into the hospital basement where she wandered alone, leaving a trail of red dots for someone to follow.

"Will you come and stay with me?" she asked when she called me the next day. "I'm afraid I'll do it again."

That night, we lay side by side in beds as uncomfortable as the couch in our old apartment. It was impossible to sleep with the IV machine chirping out reminders to the nurses to change the bags of drugs, the drugs that were supposed to make her better, but which instead were making her want to go down into the basement. I still don't understand how they could have let her wander freely in the hospital. I don't recall what we talked about that night. I just remember that morning when I told her I was moving out. The red wig was pulled back into a ponytail, and Laurie smiled and said, "Okay," and I repeated, "Okay, okay, okay."

LOVE FOR WOMEN

He said, Marry me, and she said, No, I couldn't marry someone who isn't willing to eat vegetables or soft cheese.

Camembert means more to you than me? He looked like he had just swallowed some by mistake, a big triangular wedge of it stuck in his throat.

He had vegetable and soft-cheese phobias. It was so annoying! They'd only raised a toast in a French restaurant once. She buried her face in the zucchini-green couch that she'd helped him pick out. She'd helped him buy almost everything in his classic six. She'd even persuaded him that stoneware was important, and now he owned various bowls and plates of various sizes for various foods, most of which would never touch his lips.

Goldy, he said, petting her tangle of yellow hair, and she said, Pork Pie, and he said, Let's go running. It will make you feel better.

She hissed like a cat. She hated running, even though the year before she had placed seventy-first in the NYC Marathon. In college, she was a speedster, a girl with big thighs and below-normal body fat. She ran so fast the pink bandana holding back her unruly hair always fell out during the last mile of her cross-country races. Now she was wearing out. She could barely touch her shins, and her knees popped when she walked up stairs. Her Achilles tendons felt like old rubber bands. Running had lost its charm, but it was habit, and she enjoyed its certain perks: high metabolism and perfect calves.

It was three blocks from his classic six to the park, and she made them walk. He was wearing Princeton U, and she was wearing Tommy H, and his right hand was laced into her left hand. Neither of them wore rings.

He said, I'll give you ten bucks for every runner we pass in the park, and she said, It's done.

He laughed and looked at her with gooey eyes because that's what they shouted to close deals in his business. And, moreover, some friends of his who had married last fall on Nantucket had passed out baseball caps with "It's Done" embroidered across the front because when Matthew proposed, Oona answered: "It's done."

She got annoyed with him in the park because he was running faster than she wanted to, even though it meant they were passing loads of people, and with every person they passed, he said, Ka-ching, ka-ching. She was racking up the bucks, but she still wanted to kill him or something. He ran marathons too, though they never ran one in the same year. Competing was a strain, but so was not competing. When he ran one, she resented all the attention he received, and when she ran one, he always left for a long European business trip the next day. When they had first started dating three years ago, they had agreed to minimize the number of situations in which they directly competed since she got upset about the smallest losses, like being beat in Scrabble. She couldn't manage her competitive feelings, he said, because she was a girl, and girls couldn't leave things on the court. How essentialist of you, she had told him, and he drooped, because when she took him to the court intellectually, he knew he'd always lose.

On the east side of the park underneath the crouching-panther statue, she said, Can we please slow down for Christ's sake, and he said, At the top of the hill we can.

She ratcheted back her pace near the Metropolitan Museum, but he didn't. She had to roll onto her toes and exaggerate the swing of her arms to catch up with him. Then she sprinted ahead by a couple of steps, turned around, and said, Ka-ching, ka-ching, and he said, Double or nothing the rest of the way.

You're on, she said, and those were the last words they spoke until they hit the reservoir, where she vomited in the bushes as he stroked her sweaty back.

Good job, he said, and she tried not to gloat, even though she knew that he had probably let her win. Naturally, he was much faster than she was. At home, he took four one-hundred-dollar bills from his shiny silver money clip and handed them to her.

Two misfits at a *happening* in the Meatpacking District—that's how they'd met. Goldy had gone with friends of friends (in other words, acquaintances) with the goal of adding to her Friday night repertoire. Usually she alternated between getting tipsy with the Fast Five (whittled to three since not all of her cross-country team had shins for city sidewalks) or pretending to study great masterpieces at the Met while really sizing up her Internet date and wondering whether she should politely call it a night. On occasion, she relished going to a movie by herself, a tub of popcorn clenched between her knees, a Diet Coke with three splashes of the sugary stuff at her feet, or even staying in and reading all the serious sections of the previous Sunday's *Times.* The friends-once-removed had promised European DJs, absinthe, transcendence, but after ten minutes or so, Goldy had decided it was no different from a college kegger, except instead of beer there were watered-down bottom-shelf cocktails in red Solo cups and guys who wore as much gel and eyeliner as girls, their hair groomed into weedy lawns, and women who resembled hookers, and if not hookers, suburban good girls who had worn one dress out of the house and shimmied into another en route. If Goldy rolled up her top-of-the-knee-length skirt and unbuttoned her blouse to her sternum, she'd fit in, but what was the point? Her bra was pink, not black, and she danced with too much happy enthusiasm for the stuttering rhythms the DJ was mixing. She vowed to stay until at least 12:15 because she'd paid the cover, and she was having an experience—perhaps not the one she expected, but never mind. Closing her eyes, she tried getting into her zone, but only wound up ricocheting off a guy in Levi's and a too-big button-down. He had a way of smiling that was like winking, but without one iota of creepiness.

How are you supposed to dance to this? she asked him three times before he motioned her toward the door. It was less a real question than a rhetorical one, since he danced just as badly as she did. After getting their hands stamped with red skulls that quickly bled into blobs, they stood outside in the smelly summer night and talked, one coincidence piling on top of another, the way they do when you're starting to like someone.

Let's grab a drink someplace else, he said, and she said, Sure, though once they reached the bar—a grown-up place with red banquettes and frosted globes of yellow light—Goldy was taken aback when Pork Pie slapped down a hundred for their cocktails. I'll pay, she protested, and he said, Looks like I beat you to it, and she said, But I'm a feminist, and he just laughed.

Later on, he'd claim he made the first move, and she'd protest, saying, Who talked to who first? They liked to argue about this almost as much as they liked telling people the story of their beginning. Goldy used the word *improbable*, and Pork Pie called it *lucky*, and they both secretly considered it *fate*. And aside from his vegetable and soft-cheese phobias and his avoidance of dark, difficult movies and her constant competitiveness and occasional moodiness (which made her crave the sort of dark, difficult movies that gave her an excuse to cry), they were pretty happy. So fate, yes. Maybe.

She said, See you tonight, and he said, Knock 'em dead, Goldy, before the subway doors slid together, and the train whisked him downtown to Wall Street.

She worked in poor-man's land in the Garment District, where morning, noon, and night she dodged the rack pushers shepherding the fancy outer skins of women up curbs, around puddles, and through herds of cabs. She wore the clothes they pushed—DKNY, Miu Miu, and Helmut Lang—thanks to the generosity of Pork Pie. Her wallet was lined with Thomas Jeffersons from their ridiculous bets, her body was clothed with surprise Saturday shopping sprees, the odd anniversary present marking the 127th day since their first date, the gifties he bought just because business was good, foreign derivatives were strong, he'd called Brazil, or won $10,000 in the football pool at work. He had her squirreling away all her extra money in the most aggressive mutual fund around. She could afford to be aggressive because she was young.

She stopped at the Broadway Deli, three blocks west of Broadway, for fried egg and sausage on a roll, a cup of watery coffee. Light with two sugars, she told the aproned man. Gracias. She walked up Eighth Avenue, underneath the permanent scaffolding and past the stores that sold ninety-nine-cent T-shirts and the Cuban restaurant where she bought a plate of yellow rice and black beans with fried plantain on the side from the roly-poly ladies who asked, The usual, Guapa? No variety, Guapa? You wanna try the pollo con ajo, Guapa? Muy rico. Ricisimo. She liked this neighborhood. When she had moved to New York five years before, there had still been lots of neighborhoods like the Garment District. She could remember the thrill of wandering around Alphabet City as if she were an intrepid explorer. That was the thing about New York. It prolonged the period of disorientation, of being lost, of giving you the opportunity to make magical discoveries, like the shop that sold cupcakes topped with dollops of pastel frosting on Ninth. On Ninth Avenue of all places! She didn't especially care for cupcakes, but the fact they were sold on Ninth Avenue next to a stinky bodega made her love them. She took a sip of her watery coffee.

A guy pushing prom dresses the color of blue carnations said, Let me love you, Sugar. Let me put a smile on your face.

This was the one thing she didn't like about the neighborhood. These guys, these heathens, these assholes who interrupted her walk from the subway. She looked straight ahead, pretending not to hear him, but thinking, Bastard, fuck you, fucker.

She felt breathless. Blood rushed to her temple. She was already angry, and it wasn't yet nine o'clock. It was bad enough when she reached her office (which housed sweatshops on all of its floors except for hers) and suffered the daily humiliation of walking into the lobby where the lobby guys, chain-smoking menthols, would have a poker game going with the less familiar building guys.

Every day it was the same thing. As she waited for one of the three crappy, slow elevators, they stopped their game and licked their lips, like she was a mysterious parcel tied up with string that might contain something they wanted to sample. She didn't even think she was pretty. No, that wasn't true. Rather, she tried not to think in terms of categories like pretty or not pretty, because once you began, you were your face, your pores, your hair—including the curly black ones that sometimes appeared in places other than your private areas. You were your crooked pinky, your pomegranate breasts, your sandpaper elbows, your vino belly, your thighs with half a cantaloupe scooped out beneath the hip. Then it was inevitable. You wanted to keep your pomegranate breasts but trade your butt for something more melon shaped, and you wanted to hack off your left ear, which stuck out, and could the right cream or a couple of slices of cucumber restore elasticity under your eyes? When Pork Pie told her she was beautiful, she told him to shut up, because she didn't want to consider it.

One morning after they'd been dating for just over two months, she was sunbathing on the deck of his share, and he waltzed out after sleeping until noon and sang, There's my golden girl, my lovely, my Goldy, and she shrank back from his silliness, a little happy, a little mortified, but mostly strangely self-conscious in the pink bikini she'd bought for this, her first trip to the Hamptons. And then she did that terrible thing she was apt to do when she was feeling embarrassed. She struck back: Oh hi, Pork Pie. But he just smiled and said, Hmm. Pork pies. I'm hungry. How 'bout breakfast, Goldy? And she said, Sounds good, Pork Pie. He was often oblivious to her sarcasm. It saved their relationship but could also be cat-claws-scratching-nice-upholstery maddening.

Now, she looked down at her feet to avoid the men's eyes, but mostly to resist saying something inappropriate or inviting. She wasn't even wearing a skirt. She hadn't worn a skirt in more than three weeks. The elevator car smelled like a dirty ashtray, and by the time she stepped into the office of the not-for-profit organization—or the not-for-pleasure organization, as her best office friend and lunch buddy, Anne, called it—she was so tightly wound that she wanted a cigarette and began to plot how she could bum one from the graphics guy without pissing him off. Of course, the graphics guy was the only one who smoked openly. Everyone else was too uptight or virtuous, including her.

The not-for-profit had been forced to move after a developer decided to convert its downtown digs into a luxury hotel. The real estate market was like a runaway train, the headlines screamed. She rented a room for $1,450 per month in a loft with a pressed-tin ceiling and a view of Delancey Street gridlock. The other rooms were occupied by three twenty-three-year-old guys who left crumbs on the counters. It was really just a faux chambre, or FC, a means for her to avoid admitting that she spent almost every night in Pork Pie's classic six on a quiet street lined with real trees.

She was glad they had moved, even though their new office windows offered a panorama of bolts of fabric on one floor and women hunched over sewing machines on another. After all, it was a not-for-profit, and it had always seemed wrong to work downtown amid armies of bankers. The space itself could have been a little nicer, or at least more conducive to productivity.

Converted space was how Anne described it. Translation: no hot water in the bathrooms, no carpets to absorb the echo, no shades on the windows, no heat except from the radiators along the wall, which roasted the unfortunate ones who happened to sit near them. Unfortunately, all of it was true, and she was one of the unlucky few to sit by both a window and a radiator, and on sunny winter days she felt like she was locked in a car in a parking lot in Tucson, Arizona, in the middle of the summer.

Anne had sent out an officewide e-mail that said: Unwashed Hands: How Germs Spread. Most of the women kept small bottles of liquid sanitizer in their top drawers. The ones who should have been killing germs, given their anatomical architecture, appeared unconcerned, however, and Anne started a rumor that the president and founder of the organization was going to disseminate a memo re: It's Time to Take Important Matters into Hand: What You Take into Your Hands Matters! It was rather too wordy for Elizabeth, the president, who believed that, as a rule, the subject lines of memos should be no longer than five words.

Goldy—her real name was Frances—sat down and shuffled a pile of papers from one spot to another on her desk before she powered on her computer and dug into her day's work: writing a strategy memo pitching their program to the Yetman Foundation. Their not-for-profit-nor-for-pleasure was called Pencils Are Important and Necessary Tools (PAINT), and their mission was to raise money for school supplies, including pencils, paints, pens, rulers, glue, tacks, calculators, crayons, and so on. Yetman, of course, earmarked its grant money for the arts, so in the "Likelihood" section, Frances typed *improbable.* Improbables, however, were her favorite challenge—how to persuade foundations and corporations that cared not one whit for public education, or whether schoolchildren in the Mississippi Delta had pencils, to make a commitment to school supplies. It tapped her creativity. She knew exactly how they'd pitch this one—they'd request funds for recorders. A travesty it was that elementary schoolchildren in poor, backward areas weren't learning how to play "Twinkle, Twinkle Little Star" and other favorites. Of course, they'd also throw in money for chalk and paper for copying sheet music, meeting two needs with one proposal. Her fingers danced over the keyboard.

Writing grants wasn't what Frances had set out to do. When she graduated from college, she had wanted to do something good with a capital *G,* like working with poor or oppressed women. In college, she'd been an anthro major—at her school the administration looked down upon the study of anything practical like education or social work or even business—but she'd taken a slew of courses in women's studs: *Women: Sex or Gender?*; *Gender: An Anthropological Perspective*; *Heterosexuality: "The Unconscious Non-Choice"*; and *The Economics of Marriage.* For a while, she had even considered becoming a lesbian, at least for political reasons. In spite of what her parents argued—they urged her to cash in on the value of her education—she took a job at a battered women's shelter, thinking she'd become the Jonathan Kozol of poor women, writing moving books that shed light on their plight. But the shelter was poorly run, and because of her liberal arts background, she was only qualified to work as a front desk receptionist for a salary that barely covered her rent. She had looked around—so many of the places like NOW tackled the struggles of American women who already had good jobs but wanted equal pay or needed rocks to shatter glass ceilings, or women in faraway places like Burundi and Bangladesh who were forced to consent to genital mutilation. But there was no Women's Defense Fund, no Women's Aid Society; there were just millions of poor children, children who appeared to be orphans. It was as if their poor mothers had been carefully rubbed out of the picture with erasers provided by PAINT and other not-for-profits.

I like it, Elizabeth said, and Frances said, I'm so relieved.

Though there are some changes I'd like to make in terms of wording, Elizabeth said. First, I don't like *travesty.* I don't know. It just sounds too melodramatic to me. Let's try *tragedy* and see whether that works. She tilted back in the donated office chair and put her Prada loafers on her desk.

Frances admired the shoes, the way they deconstructed

the traditional loafer with their clunkiness. Elizabeth's husband's family had money, which was what enabled both of them to work at not-for-profits and still be fashionable. Elizabeth's husband's nonprofit raised money to send new and donated eyeglasses to people in third-world countries, some of the same places where Pork Pie—whose real name was David—made his money second-guessing the rise and fall of currency values.

It is a tragedy that children in the birthplace of jazz graduate from elementary school without learning to play the recorder, Elizabeth read aloud.

Frances nodded.

Yes, I think that's better, Elizabeth said. Now let's look at *graduate*. Do elementary schoolchildren graduate? She stared quizzically at Frances, but before Frances could answer, Elizabeth punched Harry's number, even though he was just on the other side of the four-foot-high cubicle wall.

Graduate, Elizabeth said. What do you think, Harry? *Graduate* or *leave*?

Frances noticed that Harry needed no explanation. He had probably been eavesdropping on the whole discussion.

On the one hand, Harry said, *graduate* might be confusing, and on the other, *leave* is so lackluster. What about trying *emerge*? He lowered his voice: It is a tragedy that children in the birthplace of jazz emerge from elementary school without learning to play the recorder.

He's so brilliant, Elizabeth said in a stage whisper loud enough for Harry to hear over the partition.

Frances felt nauseated. Harry was one of only three men

who worked at PAINT. The other two men, the graphics guy and a new program assistant, were soft-spoken and slightly effete compared with Harry, who left the top two buttons on his Oxfords undone, revealing a triangle of tangled chestnut-colored hair. It was difficult to find men who wanted to work at not-for-profits, which made Harry very precious for the sake of workplace diversity.

The nice thing about using *emerge* is that it picks up on the birthplace language. Harry's voice boomed over the speaker-phone while echoing in the carpetless converted space. We could take the whole birth motif a step further by using "are *borne*." It is a tragedy that children in the birthplace of jazz are *borne* from elementary school without learning to play the recorder.

What about parental rights, Elizabeth asked. Aren't we skating on muddy ground?

Harry chuckled. You're a genius. It never occurred to me, but you're right on the ticket.

Elizabeth shook her head. I'm no genius, Harr. We're a good team, that's all.

Frances looked down at her notes, and for the second time that morning, she felt anger surging through her veins.

David called as Frances was drafting a thank-you note to the Peter Pan Foundation for its gift of $5,000 for movie posters (and pushpins, tacks, and tape to affix them and other items). Marry me, he said, and she said, How's the market? How many millions did you win today?

Earn, he corrected, earn.

Earn, she repeated. I can't keep it straight when you're earning and when you're gambling.

We could go to Vegas and throw a big party afterward?

What's a party without a wedge of melted Brie and crudités with creamy dip?

He gasped.

Hard day? she asked.

I'm sorry, he said, I can't think about vegetables and soft cheese right now. The bottom just fell out of the Russian bond market. We covered our margins, but who knows how we'll come out in the long run.

Oh, Pork Pie, I'm sorry. Are things terribly tense down there?

They're fine for now, he answered. How's the not-for-money business? Did you pitch the Yetman memo to Elizabeth?

Yes. It went well enough—just the usual wrangling over words, she said, sighing and fiddling with her PAINT pencil, which she had filched from the donor gift drawer. She could leave PAINT, say good-bye to Elizabeth and Harry, and no, thank you, to their inane suggestions. That would give her certain satisfaction, but moving up the ladder only meant moving on to an arts organization where, if she were lucky, she would manage an individual donor campaign, keeping track of the board's friends and producing monthly reports on their generosity. Everyone loved the arts; no doubt she would double her salary. She sighed again.

Why don't you buy yourself something nice to celebrate? Pork Pie suggested. You haven't already spent your winnings from the race, have you?

I guess I could, she said, but it seems premature. The proposal's not even out the door yet.

Don't be silly, he said. Look, I've gotta go. See you tonight, little one?

Love, she said, and he said, Ditto.

For two dollars, the graphics guy said, and Frances said, You've got to be kidding.

Why don't you just buy your own pack, he said, turning back to his screen, where he was redesigning the PAINT stationery for the third time that year. You can afford it. Your boyfriend's an i-banker.

What's that got to do with anything? Whose boyfriend's not an i-banker around here?

Mine isn't. The graphics guy still refused to turn and look at her.

He's a lawyer, Frances said. That's practically a banker, and it's certainly close enough to share your cigarettes.

Look, the graphics guy said, spinning around and facing her, he's a lawyer, but he works for Legal Aid. Heard of them? They make less than we do, and most of them are in big-time debt from law school. I'm not fucking money.

She didn't know what to say, twisting her diamond earring out of nervousness.

Point taken, she said at last. I owe you a pack. What do you want?

Spirit of America, he answered.

After buying the cigarettes, Frances walked around the block to clear her head. She wouldn't smoke. Pork Pie would tsk-tsk her if he found out and challenge her to a reservoir race. She would regret each illicit cigarette, feeling every day of her twenty-seven years. You're a real dumbo, he would say after beating her soundly, and because those were the meanest words he spoke, she would feel like crying and need to sink her thumbnail into her palm to distract herself.

The sky was gray and heavy overhead, and the pounding in her temple had not subsided. She felt dizzy. She pushed her sunglasses to the crown of her head and closed her eyes for several seconds. When she opened them, there was a rack pusher standing in front of her. She hadn't heard the rattle of his approach. He licked his lips and smiled crookedly. For once, she didn't automatically flip her sunglasses back down over her eyes. She stared at him, meeting his gaze, letting her eyes move up and down him as his moved up and down her. He was small and wiry, and his red T-shirt stuck to his chest with perspiration. His jeans were tight and frayed at the cuffs, and at the crotch she noticed an unfamiliar bulge, unfamiliar because she never let her eyes fall on the crotch of a man. Nestled up, it was the size of a big apple. She heard him laugh.

Ice Queen, he said, let pappy stick you his hot rod, and she said, What's on the rack.

BCBG, baby, the spring collection.

I'll fuck you for the blue dress and matching jacket.

He looked startled for a moment, and Frances felt astonished too. Her stomach twisted like a dinner napkin being crumpled and tossed on an empty chair, but she was also excited by the thought of the dress and jacket. It was like buying something on a very good sale, she told herself, even though she knew it was nothing like this at all. She wanted to try on the outfit, but there was no time for that in this transaction. Behind the garbage cans, she said and nodded toward the alley. Come on.

She saw that he wasn't boasting when he said he had a rod. Yes, it was a rod, and pushed up against the brick wall with her pants around her ankles and his callused hands around her waist, she closed her eyes and met his thrusts. It hurt. There was little excitement in the exchange until it was completely over—and she was fingering the rayon dress and jacket as she hurried back to the office.

That night, David met her at the door with a glass of white wine. They toasted, their crystal tinkling like a window shattering, or real birds singing on real trees outside David's apartment on the first day of spring, or both.

He said, Marry me, Goldy, and without hesitation, she said, Yes, Pork Pie! Yes!

TEMPORARY

On Monday, Vita wears a khaki-colored wool suit (Jones New York, $90) with a double-breasted jacket that has linebacker-size shoulder pads and a straight skirt that rides dangerously low on her nonexistent hips. Her roommate, Mel, comes out of her room in a sheer floral nightie that Vita covets. Vita envies almost everything about Mel, including her blunt-cut pageboy, her entire wardrobe, and her skill at flirting. Mel is as good at picking up guys as Vita is at getting job interviews. The only thing that Mel has that Vita doesn't want is a big rack.

Breasts are spiritually heavy, Vita thinks; they are for grown women, and she is just twenty-three with a top-notch degree from a fancy school and a few awards.

"Lose the shoulder pads." Mel has a real job and doesn't have to be at work until ten.

"I can't. They're sewn in," Vita says helplessly.

"Then cut them out."

"I don't think they're that bad."

"Oy," Mel says, disappearing into the bathroom. "You look like . . ." The toilet muffles the rest of what is likely a snarky remark. But Vita doesn't care—this is a good uniform for investment banks and hedge funds, where she has been temping for the past couple weeks. At places of high-stakes finance, it is useful to pretend to be as harmless as a librarian or a houseplant. It is also helpful to be a quick study of complicated phone systems and difficult, nearly unpronounceable names: Wojciechowski, Desmerais, Fuchs, Inoue. The men at investment places are mostly nice, if not a little dull, but they can't be blamed, since they spend sixteen hours a day tinkering with spreadsheets to assess the value of intangible things or converting dollars to pesos to francs to yen in such a way as to generate small percentages of profit on big piles of money.

She has learned that Kronenbourg is a beer, and the dinar was the currency of Yugoslavia. Also: bankers entertain themselves by making bets on the usual manly pastimes like football and basketball, and then on wildly stupid things like whether someone can drink a whole water cooler in a single day or eat a stick of butter in under an hour. (The answer is no. She discovered a half-gnawed cube in the break room refrigerator. Teeth marks on butter are like hair in salads. Surprisingly disgusting.) Any glimmer of interest that Vita had in investment banking has been swept into a dustpan. It's a locker room of nerds ruled by real loud assholes and human calculators, and let's face it, Vita earned a middle-of-the-road B in intro econ.

A guy—not her boss; her boss is a married man with curly red hair—flings a copy of the *WSJ* across her desk while she is organizing receipts for an expense report. Tiny slips of paper whirl to the floor, not that the guy notices.

"Look, my deal made the front page of the second section," he booms.

"That's cool, Ted." She knows his name because he is one of the few men with whom she has personal exchanges. She feels shy around him because she finds his tiny German-style glasses a little sexy, and unlike all the other guys in their dry-cleaned and cuffed Dockers, starched white shirts, and razor-cut helmet hair, he wears fancy jeans. "How was your weekend?"

He sighs and fiddles with his gold-plated fountain pen. This is what they all do when asked about their weekends, which, as a rule, are nothing more than a continuation of the week. Confronted with this question while they're sitting at their desks, they take sudden interest in their collections of Star Wars figures and water pistols.

"You're not missing much," she offers. "Ebert says this is the worst year for movies."

Vita mostly likes temping. It's like being in the witness protection program. Every week, and sometimes every day, brings a new placement where no one knows her, where no one knows that she graduated summa and won a slew of awards from the history department, and no one is disappointed in her decision not to go to graduate school. It's a good way to test her mettle, to find out who she is apart from what she has accomplished, and whether people will like her for what she can learn on the fly and not what she has the potential to be. She has been a file clerk, a secretary, an admin assistant to the head of marketing at New York Road Runners; a receptionist at a private equities firm where they have Picassos and Mirós and carpet so plush you can't hear yourself walk; an assistant's assistant (talk about power); and a nerve soother and doer of simple calculations in the employee stock purchase plan at a company preparing to merge with another. ("The basic idea is your one share of X will become one-half of Y," she tells person after person, and most respond with some variation of *Oh my God! You're a genius!*, which is both alarmingly flattering and simply alarming.)

The only problem with temping is that Vita is a terrible typist. At Kelly Girl, the first temp agency where she tried out, she did so poorly on the typing test, they told her she wasn't qualified for secretarial stints. "But there's always a demand for good receptionists," the job specialist explained before handing her a banana. "Pretend you're answering a call."

"Now do you regret not taking typing back in high school?" her mother chided during her weekly parental check-in. "Everyone should be able to fall back on typing when they decide to waste their college education." She could hear her father chuckling in the background.

The other problem with temping is not with temping per se but with work itself. School taught her the world was full of possibility, revelations, complexity in more shades of gray and gray black and white gray than you could imagine. Freud estranged her from herself, Marx made her feel like a tool (especially at her fancy, class-perpetuating school), and the postmodernists took a mallet to language. A sentence of Mary Rowlandson's captivity narrative, the subject of her senior thesis, could be read a multitude of ways. Was Rowlandson happy among the Indians who dragged her from her home, her teapots, and her children? Did she secretly want to sleep with them? Or did she find their way of life savage, their worship of many gods not only confusing but the work of the devil? Almost ditto for Vita, except her captors are client-relationship supervisors and risk managers and strategizers (the best of them product-agnostic!). The problem with temping is that Vita may wind up with no people at all: if not history, then what? If not the "real" world, then the "realer" one? The analogy explodes bit by bit.

What do people do? That's what Vita wonders at 9 a.m. on Wednesday at a midsize midtown company that specializes in consolidation while she shadows the temp supervisor (not a temporary herself) through a maze of workstations. She is wearing a coral-colored pencil skirt (a hand-me-down from generous Anna) and a short-sleeved black sweater with pearl buttons. The skirt's matching jacket hangs in her closet gathering dust because it's too much color for New York.

"I coordinate our temporary needs," the temp supervisor explains as Vita nods enthusiastically. "You can't imagine how many temps we use, not that we have high rates of absenteeism, but with vacations and special projects and our generous family leave policy, we use temps all the time."

The office is a stormy sea of grays and blacks.

"Right now, in fact, we're in the middle of a cost-benefit analysis to determine whether it would be more cost-effective to create our own permanent in-house temp pool." The woman smiles. "This is you," she says, gesturing to a desk separated by a low gray partition from a glassed-in corner office with closed venetian blinds that suggest deep REM. "I'm not sure what time Dom usually comes in, but I'm right over there." She gestures to a cubicle with a well-tended fern balancing at an intersection of partitions. The fern looks real, but Vita can't be sure. "You brought a book, didn't you? If I were a temp, I'd read all the time."

"Yeah, I mean yes," Vita says. Lately she has been trying to weed casual speak out of her corporate vocabulary. "I have a book on business."

The woman brightens. "That's terrific. We have so many temps who aren't really interested in what we do."

What do you do? Vita wants to ask but doesn't for fear of being disappointed.

"I think they're all aspiring actors and artists who temp because, you know, those are hard businesses to break into."

The temp supervisor, whose name Vita has already forgotten, gives her head a sad little shake. "Anyway, Dom may have an external meeting for all I know. Let's see . . . Maybe June, his permanent girl, left you something." She scans the desk, but it's as clean as freshly poured concrete. "I don't suppose so, since she's out with the flu. Well, in any case, make yourself comfortable."

While waiting for her boss, a VP in HR, she pretends to read *Built to Last,* a book on best business practices that Ted told her *will make you see what it's all about.* In fact, she has simply removed the jacket wrapper from the business book and put it on a novel about emancipated slaves who are themselves slaveholders. It is a fascinating read because the author presents research (census records, quotes from expert historians, journal entries, and so on) that he admits to fabricating. Vita looks up from a description of the slave quarters and watches people move purposefully back and forth from hallway to office, from break room to elevator bank, their expressions urgent. Consolidation? Shrinking? Human resources? Hiring and firing? A man in a three-piece suit saunters toward her cubicle, his unhurried pace making him look distinguished. Straightening, Vita hides her book in her lap.

"Hi?" she says.

"I'm Dom," he replies. "And you're?"

"Oh, I'm Vita. I'm your temp."

"Hi, Vita." He extends his hand. His palm is pleasingly soft, his grip reasonable. "Let me get myself settled, Vita, and then we'll see what there is for you to do."

Through the blinds, Vita can see the outline of Dom sitting at his desk. He is very still. After a bit, she knocks on his closed door. "Coffee?" she calls out.

"Come in," he says.

She has caught Dom in midthought, a red pencil hovering over a yellow legal pad. Otherwise his desk is as blank as the front of an obsessive-compulsive's refrigerator. "Do you need anything?"

"I need everything," he says, "but some coffee will do. And you can type up these."

At noon, Dom emerges from his office, an umbrella in one hand, an overcoat in the other. "I've got a lunch meeting until two. Can you hold down the fort?" He hands her a sheaf of papers. "If you're not too busy, maybe photocopy these for me?" He taps the umbrella on the floor three times. "Until soon, Vita. Until soon."

The hours unfold slowly. She photocopies the stuff Dom left behind—sheaves of country western music: "Drop Kick Me, Jesus, Through the Goalposts of Life"; "More Than a Memory"; "Size Matters"; "When the Stars Go Blue." She sharpens all the pencils in his "Country Western Rules" mug. She entertains the idea of raising his blinds and washing his windows, but she supposes this is someone else's job. She calls Anna. It's funny that she's in touch with Anna but not Sylvie, especially since there was a time when she vowed never to consort with Anna again. But Anna has turned out to be a home away from home: a purveyor of big, crunchy salads, mostly nonjudgmental job advice, tips on sample sales and dry cleaning and air conditioners.

"Hey," Vita says. "I'm so bored."

"Who's this?" Anna asks.

"Ha, ha," she says.

"Today's spy mission?" Anna asks.

"Gray cubicleland."

"Duh. I mean, what company?"

"Shrink and Slash."

Anna laughs. "It's called work for the same reason blow jobs are called blow jobs. They blow. Just get used to it."

"Ugh," Vita says. "You're so inspiring. Not."

"Oh, Vi," Anna says, "get on with it already."

When Dom comes back, she hands him the stack of photocopies. Each song (including the original) is paper clipped and organized alphabetically by title.

"You're a good worker, Vita," he says.

She doesn't know whether to wilt or blossom.

That night, Vita is reorganizing her closet when her phone rings.

"Vita?" a male voice asks.

She wonders whether it's Eric, a guy from college whom she recently bumped into at the gym. They weren't friends before, but now the fact that they're alumni of the same school and living in the same twelve-block radius seems like reason enough to buddy.

"Hello," she says.

"It's Ted."

"Ted?" she says while thinking, *Ted!* "How did you get my number?"

"One of the girls in HR sold it to me."

"What?" she squeals. She's pretty sure it's against company policy to give out private information.

"Just joking. We're friends, and Deborah, that's her name, knows that I'm . . ." he trails off. "Anyway, I'm doing a really big deal."

"That's really super," she says. "Are you still at work?"

"Yep, but I think it might make the front section of the *Journal*."

"Wow," she says, "Yay!"

There's silence, then they both start to speak at once.

"What?" she says.

"Never mind," Ted says. "I should get back to work."

"Well, don't work too late." This sounds like something her mother would say. "Ted?"

"Yes?" he asks.

"Um, well, good-bye."

"Good night, Vita."

The following Tuesday, Vita has a job interview with a trade publication that puts out newsletters with titles like "The Secondary Loan Market" and "Derivatives Today." She is still working for Dom, though to call it work is a stretch. He occasionally waves her into his office to take dictation.

"Let's see." He moves around to a second chair on her side of the desk. He steeples his hands. His fingernails are lovely ovals. "Pursuant to the employee policy manual updated and revised September 1, 2008, performance reviews shall be executed . . ."

She appreciates that he's aware of the power dynamic involved in keeping the desk between them. Professors who barricaded themselves behind their navy blue book-towered desks used to irk her. Since she doesn't know shorthand, she abbreviates: *Purs. Emp man updtd & rvsd* . . . "Can you please repeat the date?"

He raises an eyebrow, repeats the date, forges ahead. Her hand cramps into a parenthesis by the end. "Knock 'em dead at the interview," he says before dismissing her. "Be yourself, and you'll wow them. Just don't let them hire you on the spot."

Interviewing is just another form of temping, of auditioning different professional identities. Using this method, she has already ruled out public relations (too airy) and publishing (too grim). The managing editor, a guy named Leo, shows her into his office. After the usual rigmarole in which Vita answers questions about her experience (all from the college newspaper, but valuable nonetheless) and asks questions about the company (she's done her homework) and Leo's experience (people love to talk about themselves), Leo says there's one more thing. "We like to see how people work under pressure. Are you up for reporting a story?"

The hypothetical is this: rumors are flying about a big

M and A deal, and Vita's job is to nail down the details. Leo gives her a list of sources (who are actually other reporters) and shows her to a desk. She pulls down the skirt of her little knit suit (Banana Republic, $55), a friendlier shade of green than the Jones New York number, which feels risky because it is not two sizes too big for her. Her bare knees feel naked, but she doesn't do nylons. Once settled, she begins dialing numbers.

"Is this off the record?" asks a source after she's finished her spiel.

"Yes," she answers a bit too hastily, because when another source says, "I can only confirm your story if you tell me where you got your information," she is caught in a quandary. Anonymous sources seem no better than gossips. If you're not willing to stand by your word, how reliable can you be? After a split second, she outs her first source, gets the confirmation she needs, and then begins the painstaking process of writing the story. The thing that prevents her from being a faster typist is not hand-eye coordination, but slow cognitive function. She'd type as fast as a bullet train if her brain processed information faster. But alas. Historians ruminate.

"That's a good line." Leo is reading her article while she fiddles with the bottom button of her jacket. " 'This merger will result in a Taj Mahal in the building sector.' A little hyperbolic, but I like your creativity."

Vita smiles hopefully.

"You did fuck up in one major way."

"I did?" Her mouth goes dry.

"Reynolds told me that you gave up your anonymous

source." He takes off his glasses and rubs his eyes. This is either melodramatic or weary. "You never out a friend."

"I'm sorry," she says. "I just assumed . . . I don't know . . . that an anonymous source isn't super reliable, and you can't build a story around one? That was our policy at school."

"This is the real world," Leo continues, "and in the real world people's asses are on the line all the time, but especially when they pass on information you shouldn't have. Let me tell you . . ." He pauses, looking down at her résumé. "Vita, anyone who's anyone around here has only gotten there by cultivating reliable inside sources. By being discreet. By being a good friend."

"I'm sorry," she says again. "Is he going to be okay?"

"Who?"

"My inside source?"

For a split second he stares at her. Then he laughs. It sounds like barking. "You're funny."

She smiles, as though she's a person capable of telling jokes when in truth the story has sucked her into its vortex, its hold so tight she has momentarily forgotten that it's fabricated. Plus: she can't stand making mistakes, even fictional ones. Plus: this is a job interview. Criminy.

"I'll be in touch," Leo says, standing and offering his hand.

"Thanks," she says, thinking she needs to cultivate a firmer grip. "I know I made a mistake, but I think I'd make a great reporter."

Later that night when Mel staggers through the door, Vita has a Caprese salad waiting, a bottle of chardonnay missing one modest glass chilling in the refrigerator. Buying wine still gives her a little thrill.

Mel kicks off her shoes and falls on the futon they both pitched in to buy so that their small apartment could accommodate out-of-town guests. A disadvantage of having a real job is late hours. She pinches the top of her nose between her thumb and finger.

"Tough day?"

"You don't want to know." Mel does something in marketing that Vita has no interest in understanding. Does this signal something objectionable about Mel? About Vita? About their friendship? "It was majorly bad. How was yours?"

"I had an interview." She tries not to sound depressed, even though she is beginning to think that soon her desire to update her wardrobe will make her cave in like a mine shaft or a cheaply built tract house. She pours Mel a jelly jar of wine. "Voilà."

"Sweetheart," Mel says, "was it bad?"

"Honey," Vita jokes back, "I fucked up majorly."

They clink their glasses.

"Well, I heard about a job you couldn't fuck up," Mel says.

Vita perks up. She can't help herself, even though she and Mel have been through this routine a couple times before. "Really?"

"This guy is looking for a professional girlfriend."

Vita laughs. "What? A hooker?"

"No!" Mel says. "Are you kidding?"

"You want me to sell myself? Make my status as a commodity explicit? There's nothing wrong with that. I mean, I support the legalization of prostitution . . ."

"That's not what I mean." Mel takes a sip of her wine. "This guy is a European businessman, and he, like, needs a professional plus-one."

"I think that's called an escort." Is Mel for real?

"It's not like that. It's more like when I have a date with someone who skeeves me out, and you come along to make things easier. To keep it on the up-and-up. It's like a professional good friend."

Vita realizes she is fiddling with her zipper. "And I'd get paid for this?"

"You'd get compensated."

"Compensated? You really know how to wrangle with the English language."

"Oy. Conjunction, junction, what's your function?" Mel sings in her high little-girl's voice. "Hooking up words and phrases and clauses."

"Very funny."

"Conjunction, junction, how's that function?"

"Stop it," Vita giggles. "That's totally irrelevant."

"Oy, Vita, I'm just teasing." She nudges Vita with her stockinged foot. "I just thought, you know, you're an adventurous girl, and this sounds like an adventure."

"Ixnay," she says. "It sounds like too much work."

"Work?! Give me a break. You'd just have to be your own charming little self."

"Very funny," Vita repeats again, which is like saying

knock it off, only a lot nicer. She moves toward the refrigerator, only five steps from the couch. "Caprese salad?" She mangles the Italian.

"Ah oui, ma chérie," Mel says. "You are the world's best roommate."

On Wednesday at five, Dom insists on taking her out for drinks "to thank you for your diligence." She tries to say no politely, since she suspects she and Dom have said all there is to say to each other at work, but he won't hear it. They go to the High Bar at the Gramercy Park Hotel. "I'll take my regular table," Dom tells the waitress. He presses his hand into the small of Vita's back and steers her through the gray suits crowding the bar. She would like to lengthen her stride to get to the table faster, but she is wearing a satin skirt with a purply abstract print (the basement sales rack, French Connection, $29) that is so straight, it restricts her movement. The back slit could be unbuttoned, but showing leg doesn't seem professional.

"What can I get you tonight?" the waitress asks.

"The usual," Dom says.

"And for you?"

"A gin and tonic?" Vita asks.

"What kind of gin?"

"Umm." She knows nothing about liquor. Or wine. Or European politics. This is why she could never be a professional girlfriend. Mastering the basics would take her weeks.

"Bombay Sapphire suit you?" Dom asks in his pleasingly low voice.

"Perfect," she fibs.

The waitress reappears with a small bowl of pleasantly salty popcorn and a dish of warm cocktail nuts with a really good ratio of hazelnuts and Brazils to peanuts. Dom's usual comes in a martini glass. They toast, and Vita does her best to look Dom in the eye and affect a sophisticated yet casual air, not that she knows how to pull this off. Dom, she learns, is a country western singer in his free time.

"One of the few African Americans in the biz," he says with a laugh. "The industry's been dominated by rednecks, but we're changing that."

"That's cool," Vita says. "Not the redneck part, but the way you're challenging the conventions. Do you perform much?"

"Here and there," he says. "What about you, Vita? What's life got in store for you?"

"Well," she says, "I'm from southern Illinois, but I went to school out here." She doesn't know why exactly, but she winds up telling him about her thesis on captivity narratives, the accounts that Europeans wrote after being captured by Native Americans. "They're part of the conversion narrative tradition," she says, aware of how earnest she sounds. "White people stray from God, and as punishment they're captured by quote-unquote heathen Indians. Then out in the wilderness and among the savages, they rediscover God, and when they finally return to quote-unquote civilization, they write these tracts about the renewal of their faith." How does anyone indicate italics without becoming repetitive?

Her drink is gone, but there's another one waiting. She usually doesn't drink much, but the popcorn has made her very thirsty.

"That's fascinating," Dom says. "You should write a book."

"I don't know. Covering significantly new ground would require a lot more research . . ."

"Or you should work at a magazine. I have some contacts, some people I could put you in touch with."

"That's really nice." This isn't the first time one of her temporary bosses has tried to help her. She's gotten lots of leads, lots of interviews, both real and informational, from people's desires to see her settled. Her un- or underemployment makes everyone nervous. "I'd appreciate that."

After draining his second usual, Dom sweeps his hand across the windows. "Look at this, will you."

The view is beautiful, especially as the lights of the buildings become visible in the darkening hours: all those offices, all those windows, all those people working late, all the industry and productivity and commitment to capitalism.

"You're from Illinois, and I'm from Oklahoma." Dom leans in, and his hand slides up her thigh. "We're both a long way from home, and we're not sure where our final destinations will be."

She doesn't understand what Dom is saying until his lips are doing something on hers, and she feels obliged to do something back. Damply excited, whether from the kiss or its public nature or the fact that Dom is her boss, she isn't sure.

"Hmm," Dom says. "I don't know what came over me."

This disappoints.

"I'm just a babe magnet." She stops, thinks. "Wait, that's not what I mean." She giggles nervously. "I mean these lips . . ." She vaguely knows she is supposed to say "I'm glad you did" or "I feel the same way," some gesture toward reciprocated affection.

His thumb finds the knob of her hip and presses. She shivers. Before she can navigate her way to a complete thought, they are kissing again.

"My place or yours?" he says, just as it's rumored to be said in the movies, though Vita herself hasn't ever seen this line delivered without irony.

"Sure," she says, as though he has asked her to bring him a cup of coffee or type a letter.

He laughs—"We'll go to my place"—hooks a hand around her waist, and reels her out into the street, where a cab waits. (Why is it they're always there when it would be better if you had to work a little harder?) Vita's need for fresh air unmet, she is still fuzzy as they head uptown. It's only when her skirt is pushed up to her knees that she's really regretting her rule against nylons—not that Dom's kisses are clumsy. He is smooth, and she is flushed and eager, even greedy, but he is also her boss, and though she has not yet established a rule in this regard since she only joined the "real" world two months ago, she thinks fooling around with bosses is probably risky, unproductive, unprofessional, plus the possibility of being a temp girlfriend seems problematic. She pulls away, sees the fringe of the cabbie's head, feels embarrassed.

"Dom, I can't do this. You're my boss."

"I can fire you." He yawns, exhaling a hint of green olives and something sharper.

"I don't know," she says.

Cupping her chin, he whispers, "You're fired, darling," and then begins to offer her generous, if not slightly distracted, severance. Still, after the cab draws in front of a brightly lit entrance somewhere on the Upper East Side, and a doorman opens up the door and good-evenings Dom, she blurts out, "I think I need to go home. I'm sorry."

"As you wish," Dom mumbles.

She thinks she hears him add, "silly young thing."

The cab half-circles the block and speeds south. Though the traffic lights of the avenue turn green all the way downtown, she still has to dig out her emergency twenty from behind her license to pay the fare.

The next morning Vita's phone rings at 7:45, and she learns that Dom really has fired her, though her job specialist doesn't say this. She says, "The temp supervisor mentioned that the VP of HR needs someone with more sophisticated secretarial skills. Did you hit a pothole taking dictation?"

After exchanging a few pleasantries, her job specialist tells her not to fret, next week is another week, but what Vita hears is that there are no new placements. In light of this, she must refigure how much money she will have by the end of the week (minus taxes), since she did not temp every day that week. Then, while Mel is perfectly accessorizing a Calvin Klein suit that she would almost kill for (that she will have to kill for if she doesn't find gainful employment soon), Vita calculates out how much money she will have by the end of the month (minus rent) if she screws up again—(instead of screwing?)—and only works three or four days a week. "That is totally effed up," Mel says to her reflection. "You should, like, totally sue."

"I know," Vita says halfheartedly. Afterward she dresses like her normal self (in jeans and a zippered black hoodie), practices typing pages from Cotton Mather sermons, reads her novel, still sheathed in *Built to Last,* and naps.

That evening, it begins to rain. The street turns a darker shade of gray, and the sidewalks are umbrellaed over. It is five o'clock, that hour when people finish one thing and start another, not quite metamorphosing. More like changing outfits. Six o'clock will release another wave. Seven, yet another. And so on and so on throughout the night. Leo calls and offers her a job covering the secondary loan market. Ted calls and doesn't quite ask her out.

"I got a job offer at Corporate Investor Publications."

"No way!" Ted booms. "That's great. Did you take it?"

"Not yet."

"Well, what are you going to do?" he presses.

What will she do? If nothing changes, on Monday and Tuesday she'll temp at Condé Nast, where everyone is scary thin, interesting looking though not terribly attractive, and they want coffee all the time. At some companies, they have desks that are plainly meant for temps—they're like Super 8 motels: just necessities and no indulgences—but at Condé Nast, hers will clearly belong to someone else. She'll study a picture of two men, wondering which one of them works there. Hard to tell. They're both young and impossibly hip, the way gay guys are. Their smiles are practiced, a little impish. This is something she needs to work on. In every picture, she looks a little different. On Wednesday, she'll file. On Thursday and Friday, on the switchboard at Ralph Lauren's corporate headquarters, she'll find herself adopting the faux British accent that the other temps use: "Ralph Lauren, may I help you?"

"I don't know," she says, even though she does. Her conversion, mundane and not singular, is close at hand, and she wants to savor her last few days of freedom—if such a thing exists. Her individuality is just a fiction. Who said that? All her big ideas are already slipping away. A temp is just a worker with commitment issues. She holds her breath longer than usual.

"Ted?"

"Yeah?"

"Do you wanna go out for martinis?" She almost says Bombay martinis, but she's pretty sure that's not the proper terminology.

"To celebrate?" Ted says. "You bet."

On the street, everyone is going somewhere, even if they don't quite know where. That's both the promise and the lie of the world. It would be easier if Vita didn't understand this.

"To celebrate," she says. "To celebrate."

NONE OF THE ABOVE

Who will come to my wedding?

- **A. My parents**
- **B. My brother**
- **C. My betrothed**
- **D. None of the above**

There is a spider who lives in a high corner of the big bay windows that look out on the garden. The garden is more like a nursery because all the plants are in pots, just in case

Carlos, the man who lovingly tends the garden, ever decides to move. He has lived in the apartment building for more than twenty years and looks like he would ride a motorcycle, except that his teeth hang by slender roots from his gums. I leave the spider and her web unmolested because of the fat black flies who whoosh through the bedroom window, the one I leave open for the cat, who is fond of jumping out, eating potted plants in the garden, leaping back inside, and regurgitating tangles of bright green grass on the wooden floor. When the flies get caught in the web, the spider is at the ready, climbing her jungle gym of delicate thread more expertly than the children at the elementary school beyond the garden on the other side of the high cyclone fence. The flies sound like faraway race cars, gunning their engines to hurl themselves down a straightaway or around a bend when they find themselves glued to the web with the spider poised to kill them.

My desk is pushed against the window where the spider lives. This is where I sit when I write multiple-choice questions for schoolchildren—not the schoolchildren across the garden, who, in fits of occasional anger or exuberance, throw one another's winter jackets over the high fence, but schoolchildren who live in Ohio and West Virginia and whom I will never meet:

> ***Read the sentence. If you find a mistake, choose the answer that is the best way to write the underlined section of the sentence. If there is no mistake, choose* Correct as is.**

Arnold built a ship out of toothpicks
that were three stories tall.

A. **Arnold built a ship out of, that were three stories tall, toothpicks.**

B. **Arnold, who was three stories tall, built a ship out of toothpicks.**

C. **Arnold built a ship that was three stories tall out of toothpicks.**

D. **Correct as is.**

I feel sorry for the children who have to answer these questions. I am told that if they do not apply themselves to the study guides I write, they will fail important tests and get held back. Imagine flunking fifth grade because you can imagine a three-story-tall Arnold, a towering boy with delicate fingers whose hobbies include shipbuilding and farming worms. I picture him in the backyard—not the garden, but the backyard of my childhood—a half acre of land with a dead catalpa in the middle where we swung from an old tire until the day the branch came down with a crash. I see the building-tall boy stabbing electric stakes into the sod, making the ground extracharged so that the worms rise and thrust out their naked heads. I see Arnold studying the lawn through his superspy binoculars from a great height before carefully lowering himself and tweezering free the worms like the finest loose threads.

My brother, whose name also happens to be Arnold, was involved in worm cultivation, along with his best friend, Luke.

Bitten by the capitalist bug one summer, they harvested dozens and dozens of worms, storing them in an old wooden barrel in our garage. They had planned to sell them to the convenience store a half mile from our house, but the manager didn't want them, and they quickly moved on to another moneymaking scheme and forgot all about the worms. August heat sucked the moisture from the dirt, and the worms hardened into squiggles as crunchy as chow mein noodles. Now Luke is a recovering drug addict, and Arnold is dead, a casualty of the war in Iraq. So eliminate "B." Arnold will not come to my wedding, and I will not go to his. The best I can manage is test questions, the occasional imaginary Arnold doing something extraordinary. I know if Arnold took this test, he would pass with flying colors. Even though grammar was never his specialty, he would offer a quick solution to the chimpanzees slowly chattering for their bananas, not that chimpanzees are the real problem. Banana slugs are.

The chimpanzees chattered <u>slowly</u> as they watched the banana slugs creep toward the cat food.

A. The chimpanzees chattered as they watched the banana slugs creep toward the slowly cat food.

B. The chimpanzees chattered as they slowly watched the banana slugs creep toward the cat food.

C. The chimpanzees chattered as they

watched the banana slugs slowly creep toward the cat food.

D. Correct as is.

In addition to the spider, the cat, and the flies, there is a slug—not my boyfriend, the one I intend to marry despite what I imagine would be my parents' threats to stand when the minister asks, "Is there anyone who opposes this marriage?" and speak their minds. (Using process of elimination [POE], you would be making a fairly educated guess if you struck my parents from the list of people who are likely to attend my wedding as well.) A slug/the slug/the slugs emerge from the crack beneath the backdoor. (It's important to note that you can use the definite article with both the singular and plural forms of the noun; the indefinite article is a different story.) This experience has taught me that slugs like to eat cat food, but cats don't like to eat slugs. When there is a slug spooned over the cat food like marshmallow fluff, my cat does nothing. She likes flies fine, but not slugs because, I suppose, there is no challenge in catching and eating them. Then the challenge is mine—to carry the dish of cat food to the garbage without tipping the slug onto my foot. The back stairs are narrow and rickety, and the thought of upsetting the slug food onto the ground and luring more slugs from the dusty corners of the basement is enough to upset me, though I do not generally upset easily. For instance, I would walk a mile sucking a lime if I could tempt Emil to marry me, but neither e-mail nor anagrams nor homophones seem to entice my betrothed-to-be to appear with a jar of daffodils, to build me a three-story picket fence. I have chosen just the spot—on the desk next to my brother's picture—to display the daffodils. I will assure Carlos that I did not steal them from his garden, though I cannot vouch for Emil, because I barely even know him. This is why my parents would oppose the marriage, and who can blame them? They are upset about Arnold, and my plans to plan a wedding before I have even secured a husband would salt their wounds. They are old-fashioned. They do not believe in green card marriages, open marriages, courthouse marriages, starter marriages, secret marriages, or marriages of convenience for insurance purposes. They do support gay marriage as long as the loving couple intend to adopt or buy sperm and a baster and get down to business.

I made that last part up. My parents, good liberals, support gay marriages with or without children. When my brother, Arnold, announced his intention to join the Marines, just shy of his twenty-seventh birthday and a year before we declared war on Iraq, they begged him to reconsider, and then when they saw how determined he was, they begged him to go back to school and earn the last three credits he needed to graduate so he would have the option of enrolling in officers' school instead of going straight into the infantry. That's not a sentence a student in Ohio or West Virginia should read, not because I'm ashamed of what my parents wanted for Arnold or what Arnold said he believed in, but because it's a run-on.

The only grammar the cat knows is the sound of a key in

the front lock, the caw of the backyard blue jay, the mechanical pop of a fresh can of Fancy Feast being opened. The blue jay sometimes alights on Carlos's shoulder while he waters or weeds the garden, its animal intuition keen to the fact that Carlos is a kind man with no interest in raiding its nest. The same can't be said for the cat, who would present herself with a hero's medal for massacring a baby bird. Arnold knew his nouns and verbs, his adjectives and adverbs. He knew, for instance, that cats do not purr brave, but that brave cats purr. He knew he could run faster and do more pull-ups and sit-ups than most twenty-one-year-olds. He knew the difference between comparatives and superlatives, knew that being *better than most* was nearly as good as being *the best.* I'm not sure whether he had considered the grammar of movement to contact or maneuver under fire. *He maneuvered under fire better than 95 percent of the other Marines.* But what about that other 5 percent? And the peculiar nature of the word *forever*?

***Don't assume there is always a correct answer. If none of the answers is correct, choose* None of the above.**

The spider lived forever, but died once.

A. The spider lived once, but died forever.

B. The spider lived forever, but died.

C. The spider lived, but died once.

D. None of the above.

If I were a student, I would lose my faith in formal education when I got to that one, and if I were brave or rebellious or overbursting with life, I would just forget about the test and make an interesting pattern with the rest of the answer bubbles. Art is as good an answer as any. As for the spider, her life span is probably shorter than a human's, but I can't be sure. Cats may linger until their early twenties, and if you're lucky enough to own a parrot, you'll have a lifelong companion. For a period of time, the spider in my window and my brother were both alive. Then I went to Boise. My parents and I had to go through Arnold's things, his LEGOs and Star Wars figures, his mechanical bank that sorted coins by weight and from which I stole quarters whenever I was short on money, his track ribbons and high school dance pictures—there he is wearing enormous glasses, there he is with a powder blue boutonniere, his arms wrapped around a girl wearing equally huge eyeglasses and a carnation pink corsage that matches her dress . . .

The name of Arnold's high school girlfriend was—

A. Liz Roberts.

B. Liza Robertson.

C. Elizabeth Robison.

D. I'm not sure.

E. I can't remember.

F. I wish I could remember.

G. I have decided that it's Lisbeth Rodgers.

He still had all the Choose Your Own Adventure books that had once been mine and a beautiful hardback version of *Goodnight Moon* that he'd sold to Luke for five dollars just before both sets of parents put an end to their commercial activities because someone was always getting gypped.

"Do you remember when he got cut from the football team?" my mother said, holding up a dusty record album with a black cover. For some reason, Arnold had gotten a real stereo with a turntable and a tape player when he was a kid. If he weren't dead, I probably would have started to joke-complain about the inequities of being the oldest.

"No," I said.

"You don't remember how he came home, and he locked himself in his room?"

"No," I said.

"How can you not remember this?" she said.

"It was a long time ago," I said. "You can't suddenly expect me to remember everything."

She didn't look like a good liberal anymore, especially when she raised her hand as if she wanted to slap me. They had a flagpole in the front yard now, but they also drove a Prius. Grief had unpredictable results.

"What?" I said.

"What what?" she said.

If you think too hard about the grammar of talking, it can fill you with despair.

"What were you telling me?"

"He listened to this album . . ." It was Pink Floyd's *The*

Wall. "He said it was so depressing it made him feel better about his own situation. It put everything in perspective." She blew her nose into a Kleenex that she had been holding for three days straight. It looked like a clump of stringy bread dough. I offered her the tiny packet of tissue I'd stuffed into the back pocket of my jeans and thought of the following: the monkeys mopped up the banana slugs' slime with their *pocket-size* tissue. Kids would get a kick out of a sentence like that, especially if one of the choices included pocket-size slime.

"That's a nice story," I said.

"It's not a story," she said, and before I could assure her that by story, I did not mean "made-up thing," she added, "It's the truth."

The cat didn't like Boise; there was so much grass she couldn't decide which blades to eat. She stopped coughing up hairballs, grew sluggish, peckish. Nothing could rouse her, not even baby squirrels. That's when I decided I should get married. We needed a to-do list that didn't involve the Salvation Army and donations to scholarship funds and candlelight vigils and trying to track down girls from junior high dance pictures who probably have enough crap and heartache in their lives already without the news of Arnold. But, of course, before I marry, I need an Emil or a Neil, an Anil or a Niles—and it is not just a matter of switching letters and choosing the right form of the indefinite article. Everything would be more auspicious if no article were necessary, but I know better than most that with hard work and discipline, you can do anything. At least, that's what I tell kids in Ohio and West Virginia.

> ***Congratulations! You've completed the practice book for the Ohio State Reading Comprehension Test, and now you're ready to race to success on the exam. To make sure your car is in tip-top shape:***
>
> ✔ ***get a full night's sleep;***
> ✔ ***eat a good breakfast;***
> ✔ ***dress in comfortable clothing;***
> ✔ ***bring three sharpened No. 2 pencils with good erasers; and***
> ✔ ***review process of elimination (POE) the night before.***

Everyone knows, though, that things happen, that the best-laid plans are sometimes ruined by surprises: the cat scrabbling around half the night with a mouse she's brought in from the garden, milk mysteriously souring in the carton, skin too tender to be touched by anything, even clothing. When I am back at my desk after my trip to Boise, I see that the spider is still there. Moreover, she has laid another purse of eggs. Because of what happened the first time (a massive explosion of tiny spiders across the window, carnage), I use a tissue from the box on my desk, pluck the package of eggs from the web, and flush the whole thing down the toilet. I avoid speculating about the spider's feelings. Even though I caution students against talismans and charms *(You make your own luck! Hard work is what it takes!)*, I cross my fingers, hoping that Carlos is not in the garden, hidden behind the boisterous clumps of calla lilies that have just unfurled their smooth white trumpets, that he will not knock on my window and ask me why I am crying not just now, but in the morning when I am drinking my first cup of coffee and just after lunch when it is too soon to go back to work and I fill the minutes with little tasks like trimming my toenails and scanning old photos and sorting paper clips by size or color and also at other moments that I cannot predict and, even afterward, do not wholly understand.

I review process of elimination (POE) one more time because perhaps there's still a slight chance that someone besides me will show up for my wedding.

POE? It's a snap!

1. *Read the question.*
2. *Read each answer carefully.*
3. *Eliminate each answer that <u>you are confident</u> is **wrong**.*
4. *Choose the best answer from the choices that are left.*

Even if you aren't 100 percent sure you know the right answer, POE can help you make

> ***an informed guess. If you guess without eliminating any incorrect answers, you have only a 25 percent chance (1 out of 4) of guessing correctly. If you get rid of one wrong answer, then you have a 33 percent chance (1 out of 3) of choosing the correct answer. If you do away with two wrong answers, then you have a 50 percent chance (1 out of 2) of being right. POE increases your odds of getting the question right!***

Is it possible that I have eliminated the wrong choices, that my guesses have not increased my odds but done the opposite, taken them down to zero? There is the church, and there is the steeple. Open the doors, and there are the people: Arnold, my mother and father holding hands, my aunts and uncles and their children, my grandparents, all dead for many years, but surprisingly real-looking ghosts. There, at the front of the tiny chapel, is my neighbor Carlos, fussing with the flowers. As usual, he is greasy. In the third pew is my best friend, Vita, whom I have seen exactly once since Arnold's death because I can manage multiple-choice questions, but not essays, and everything she asks requires an answer too long and complex for my state of mind. Grief has made me a misplaced modifier, a fragment, a ______ that is missing its subject . . .

But there is Emil! I always hoped he would turn out to be my betrothed, because of his wit, the shape of his green eyes, his strong hands and perfectly executed espresso.

An old organ starts to play the processional off-key in an

atmospheric way, and I glide down the aisle as though I have practiced walking in a long gown that I bought from Second Time Around to compensate for my natural clumsiness, until I remember that I am the one who writes the multiple-choice questions, and I know the right answers, and there is only one.

I wish I could admit to students that guessing still involves a risk, dumb luck, pretty good odds of being in the wrong place at the right time.

"Shit," Arnold said the last time I talked to him on webcam. "I almost stepped on a camel spider last night. If I'd gone to the can just a few minutes earlier . . ."

He must have recognized the look on my face, the same one I wore the time we saw a rattlesnake in the foothills above Boise. Don't believe a word of what you read about camel spiders, he told me. "First of all, they're not technically spiders, they're solpugids."

I thought, *Maybe Arnold will go back to school and study entomology when he gets out of the Marines. Maybe he will be able to explain how slugs sneak into houses. Maybe he will show me a way to live with them peacefully.*

"And they don't eat camels' stomachs, and they can't run thirty miles per hour. Yeah, they're scary as hell, but they're only six inches long. I don't know how they doctor those photos so they wind up looking as big as a man's thigh bone."

Despite the delay, which made everything Arnold said and did look jerky, I thought, *There is my brother. There he is, even though he is halfway around the world fighting a war,* and I said, "What happens if they bite you?"

He laughed. "Hurts like a bitch, but you can't die from them."

And I laughed too. "That's a relief," I said. "That's one less thing to worry about." And then, after talking some more, we said good-bye. I meant to ask him whether it's hard to tell the difference between a scorpion and a camel spider, between a car of confused civilians that fails to slow at a roadside checkpoint and a car that is racing to get as close as possible before exploding. I wanted him to tell me about some secret military strategy more effective than process of elimination, something surer than an educated guess that I could pass on to students in Ohio and West Virginia so that they would never not ace a test, so that every one of them would live happily ever after. But I didn't get the chance.

GAMES

My plan is simple: kiss Peter's ball as a means of bonking Hayley. After you kiss in croquet, you may whack the other player or take an extra stroke. I want to hit Hayley deep into the heart of the blueberry bushes so that her mallet turns blue from chipping at her ball among the ripe berries.

"Bamarama," I say, rattling the ice in my mint julep. "Take that, you playboy."

"Shit," Peter says, stretching out the word like a piece of saltwater taffy. "I guess I'm a goner."

I move my ball a mallet's length from his.

"What?" Peter says. "I'm off the hook, Sylvie?"

I aim for Hayley, and my ball smacks hers.

"You brute," she says as her ball goes spinning into the bushes.

I know it's cruel to go after Hayley, but I've been annoyed with her since the drive up from New York to Alex's parents' summer house in Maine. "I have to pee, I have to pee, I have to pee," she chanted at regular intervals, and Alex dutifully pulled over, which makes sense, I suppose, since he has the hots for her, even though she has a boyfriend named Geoff, a reclusive sculptor who's also a weekend race car driver. Alex is Peter's best friend, and Peter is my boyfriend. Hayley, as the *y* in her name suggests, is the kind of woman who always has to be the center of attention. I have this theory that the Western world is populated by two kinds of women: small women with big hair, and average to big women with all kinds of hair. Small women with big hair aren't necessarily small, but they have some quality that makes them childlike, like little-girl women. Women like this exist in a state of grace; the world still extends to them, everything for their pleasure. Even though Hayley has closely cropped blonde hair, she's clearly one of them.

"Don't be a sourpussy," Alex says before he takes his turn. "It's all fun and games until someone's whites get dirty."

"I give up," Hayley says.

"Don't," Alex says. "Just move your ball to the edge of the bushes."

"Yeah," Peter chimes in.

I look at Peter but fail to establish eye contact with him through the mosquito netting that's wrapped around the baseball cap he's wearing. We've all donned these contraptions to keep away the bugs. All Peter told me about Hayley before the trip was that she was supersmart, even though she didn't go to college. This is code for *cool* in the language spoken by Peter and Alex, who get turned on by women who read Hegel, not as well as they do, but well enough.

"Those aren't the rules." My voice sounds shrill. "You have to hit from wherever you find yourself."

"Fine," Hayley says, suddenly turning away from us and walking toward the bushes. "I can play by whatever rules."

"It's just a fucking game, Sylvie," Peter says. "We're not setting organizational policy. We're on vacation."

In the shadows of the blueberry bushes, Hayley misangles her mallet, and her ball barely moves.

"Can I just quit?" Hayley whines, but Alex is by her side, telling her she can take a do-over: "Croquet rule #256 states that ball must progress or regress by at least six inches, and if, whereby it fails, the stymied gent or lady must shoot again." He looks at me. "Agreed, Sylvie?"

"Of course." I feel myself soften a little toward Hayley.

"Have you some advice?" Alex asks Peter.

"Do you mind if I show you how?" Peter asks Hayley.

"I need all the help I can get," she says.

Peter is a master of croquet, not because he plays much, but because he is a ruthless competitor in all sports that involve using an intermediary device to hit balls. His specialty is tennis, but he can also hold his own in badminton and pool. If there were an Olympics of social games, including bridge and hearts and perhaps backgammon and debate, Peter would clean up. He hates to lose. When I once reminded him that social means sociable, he growled, "What's the point?" Then he hitched his fingers through my belt loops and yanked me toward him. "I eventually won you, didn't I?" This is true, though it didn't take much. I was pretty lost in something I still can't quite explain when Peter persuaded me to go out on a *real* date with him. "Since kissing doesn't seem to count as intent to get serious in your book," he said, "you've forced me to go old school: dinner and a movie?"

Now, I watch as Peter stands behind Hayley and wraps his arms around her so that they're standing parallel, aiming toward the ocean and the second wicket. Peter shuffles in his flip-flops, moving into position, and Hayley's clogs answer. Then he pulls back her arms, like he's setting the pendulum of a grandfather clock into motion, and the heavy ball darts through the kelly green grass like a small, furtive animal running for cover and rolls right on-target toward the wicket. A nickel-size dimple appears in Hayley's cheek. And Peter's face is stamped with a clown's grin so silly I can feel his jaw ache.

The cottage has five bedrooms, and Peter and I retreat into one at the far end of the second floor. There are mouse droppings in the box of Kleenex next to the bed. Naked under the cumulus cloud of goose down, we begin to fight.

"So," I say.

"So?"

"What was that all about?"

"What?" Peter answers.

"You know. During croquet."

"I was helping her," he says. "Why are you like this, Sylvie?" Peter opens a book the size of a cinder block on the history of New York.

"I can't believe you like people like her."

"Why?"

"Her whole Marxist critique of higher education? Her family's hardly the proletariat. How do you think she can afford to work for a photographer?"

"So?"

"She didn't go to college because she hated school."

"She's interesting."

"Give me a break. She's insipid. Were you listening to the conversation on the way up?" I slump against my pillow.

"Which one?"

"Where she said she hated high school, but sixty-seven of her classmates have friended her on Facebook."

"So what? I'm friends with people I don't even remember." Peter pretends for a moment to get engrossed in a page of his tome, which annoys me.

"She contradicts herself constantly, and she doesn't seem the least bit aware of it. She told me that until six months ago she didn't own any shoes besides combat boots. Then she started wearing clogs and Converse low tops. It was as if she experienced some profound breakthrough when she realized she could wear clogs. I wanted to shake her and say, *You're twenty-six. You can wear any kind of shoes you want.* How does Alex know her, anyway?"

"They met in Costa Rica last summer."

"And he's hoping for something to happen?"

"He'd be thrilled. I'd be too."

"I'm sure you would." I press the palm of my hand against my chin.

"Don't start. You know that's not what I mean. Kiss?" he asks.

Even though I know I should tamp down my ugly feelings, I feel them wriggling like worms in a container of fishing bait. In the past year, I've only added one new name to my list: Peter's. "Gonna get married?" Laurie teases when we chat over the phone. She has moved back home. "Gonna have babies?" I'm twenty-eight, a socially appropriate age for settling down. I love Peter, but being with someone means being with yourself in a way that's harder than when you are on your own.

"I have a tattoo," I say illogically. "Why doesn't mine count for anything?"

My tattoo is small—just the call numbers for *Clarissa* inked in neat penmanship across the lower left side of my back. I got it on a whim in Oxford when literature still felt urgent to me. The first time Peter peeled back my black wool tights, I gave him the sexy one-line summary: "It's about a coquette who's ruined by a rake." Peter laughed: "You're the thinking man's bombshell."

Now Peter answers, "Of course yours counts. But it's different. It's an allusion to a book, for Christ's sake."

"So butterflies are better?"

"Not better," he says, "just different. Stop being so competitive."

I don't move. "I don't understand how you can like someone like her and like me, too."

"I can like her, but like you differently," Peter says. "I can think she's wonderful and still love you."

I turn away.

"All right, then," Peter says. "No kiss."

But I turn back, and we begin kissing. We come up from the covers, and I straddle Peter, and we start to have sex. His face comes unmasked, and I notice the things that are pure Peter: how half of his left eyebrow has been rubbed away by worry, and how above the other is a small scar he got from jumping off the shed in his backyard when he was a child. His fine blond hair sticks up. All of this, and especially his expression—which is always stunned when we first come together—reminds me of a little boy. I press my hand against Peter's neck, gently at first, then I gradually clamp it harder between my thumb and index finger. I can feel his Adam's apple bob when he swallows. Peter likes this; he likes it when I take control. He's told me it's a turn-on, which is why I do it. Usually I loosen my grip after a few seconds, sit back on my heels, forget about how Peter looks unmasked, and concentrate on how we feel together. But tonight I don't.

Peter rasps; his expression changes. He looks at me as though I'm a stranger. I shift my weight and move my other hand to Peter's neck, my thumbs pressing in on both sides of his voice box. The flesh yields, but not the bones. His tongue comes out of his mouth, the narrow tip of it touches his top lip, and his eyes close. And then suddenly they open, both at the same time, and he says, “Stop it, Sylvie. You’re hurting me.”

“I’m sorry,” I whisper, reducing the pressure, turning my fingers into something light and without intention, like birds’ feathers. “You should have said something.”

Peter pushes himself up on his elbows until he’s sitting. He grabs my shoulders and presses me backward to the bed, and we keep having sex until he comes. Then he rolls off and faces the windows away from me, and I know that it’s over.

It’s so quiet and still when Peter speaks, his voice is like an object that trips you in a dark room.

“Why did you do that?” he demands.

“What?”

“Never mind. Good night.”

“Kiss?”

Peter doesn’t move. His back is still turned to me.

“Backs can’t kiss, can they? All right, lipless back, no kiss. I get the picture.”

The next morning, Hayley announces that she’s going to fix blueberry pancakes for everyone.

“Frowns or smiles?” she quizzes, sashaying around the enormous oak table and touching each one of us on the head with an orange-handled spatula.

“Confounded,” Peter answers.

“You mean confused?” Alex asks.

"No, more like bewildered," Peter says.

"What's the difference?" I ask.

"They're completely different," Peter replies. "Confused is more straightforward—like directions are confusing. Confounded is more like confused beyond comprehension."

"Do you know that for a fact," Alex asks, "or should we check the *OED*?"

Hayley looks from Peter to Alex. Her hair's pulled back from her forehead with a pink band, and she's wearing a long apron that says, "If you want your dinner, kiss the cook."

"You guys," she says, staring straight at me, "sound like you woke up on the anal side of the bed."

Only after hearing the second half of the sentence do I realize she's not addressing me. Instead, her look is inviting me to be her co-conspirator, her secret ally. Girls united; whatever. Peter grins, and Alex strokes his goatee, treading water in his own thoughts.

"Anal, eh," Alex says at last. "Look, we're eggheads. Got a problem with that?"

Peter cracks up first, and then Alex begins to giggle, his shoulders gently shaking. It's not that funny, but it means something to them.

Now Hayley's the one who looks bewildered. She bites her bottom lip. "Right," she says. "What's the *OED*, anyway?"

In any other situation, this kind of question would prompt Peter to say: "Oh my God." I can hear him, the way he would draw out the space between each word, aiming for the maximum dramatic effect. "Oh. My. God."

It's silent—just for a split second—but this cook is very kissable. If I asked something like that, they'd have me immediately trussed and ready to hold over the hot flames of their sarcasm.

"It's just a dictionary," I tell Hayley, surprising myself and probably Peter. "*OED—Oxford English Dictionary.* It's like a history of language."

"Sylvia went to Oxford," Alex says.

"Sylvie's very smart," Peter adds.

"Fuck off," I tell them.

"Oh," Hayley says. She's quiet for a moment.

"Where's the wand?" I say. "You've got to find out how Alex woke."

"Here." She taps him on one shoulder, twice on the head, then on the other shoulder.

"Astonished," Alex says.

Hayley narrows her martini olive–colored eyes. "You woke surprised?"

"I dreamt my arm was amputated," Alex explains.

"How?" Peter asks.

"I don't remember."

"Did you get it stuck in a thresher?" I say.

"There's our farm girl." Peter smiles at me.

"You grew up on a farm?" Hayley asks.

"Sort of," I answer, "an orchard near a small town called La Grande, Oregon."

"Cool," Hayley says.

"The dream wasn't about me losing the arm," Alex says. "In the dream, I'd already lost it, but I thought it was there."

"Of course, because it was." Peter hates talking about dreams. He thinks two people have been together too long when they start being fascinated by each other's dreams.

Alex leans back and tilts his chair onto two legs, and Hayley stands behind and kneads his shoulders.

"You had a phantom limb," I say.

"You're tense," Hayley observes.

"I was at a party on someone's terrace," Alex continues.

"Like your parents'?" Peter asks.

"Maybe. I remember looking down on the park and thinking how wild it was, how with the trees hiding everything you can imagine being alone."

"Your parents have a terrace that overlooks the park?" Hayley asks.

"My parents . . . ," Alex starts.

"His parents . . . ," Peter says.

"Eat high on the food chain," Alex finishes and laughs.

On the table are salt and pepper shakers that look like small dachshunds. The one time I met Alex's mother, she talked to her dogs more than she talked to me.

"Geoff's parents are super rich, too," Hayley says, peering into the refrigerator. "His sister's spending three hundred dollars a plate for her wedding. The only place they registered was Tiffany's."

Outside it's sunny, but an irregularly shaped shadow is

drifting across the back lawn. Peter's face looks like someone has pulled a tinted transparency over it, like a shade dimming a window.

"Geoff's parents have money?" Alex asks.

Knowing Peter and Alex, they are probably thinking that Alex's odds with Hayley aren't looking so good anymore, even though he's a social worker, which gives him the do-gooder-with-money angle. But in men's fantasies of women's romantic interests, the artist with coin is practically at the top of the pyramid, alongside the rich-as-shit cowboy. What they don't know is cowboys don't exist, not in the way that easterners imagine western men. La Grande was filled with guys who worked as hired hands on big ranches, and they all wore baseball caps and tried to put away enough money so that they could move into town and start taking classes at Eastern Oregon State College. And the ranch owners, the ones with the real money, were more businessmen and politicians than anything else.

"They're loaded," Hayley says. "But Geoff just wants to be an artist. Having money's such a burden. I'm glad my family's normal. I won't have to worry about some big wedding."

Alex looks stricken. "Are you planning on getting married soon?"

Hayley blushes. "No, I mean, whenever. Marriage is totally old-fashioned."

"I'll second that," I say.

"I'm starved," Peter says, standing up.

The topic of marriage makes all of us nervous. This summer, Peter, Alex, and I are going to five weddings of friends from college. To say you don't want to get married makes you wonder what you're doing sleeping in the same person's bed several times a week, but to say you do brings waves of despair.

Hayley moves to the stove. "I'm not exactly sure how I'm supposed to make a pancake look confounded," she says, scooping blueberries out of a bowl and dropping them into the sizzling skillet of pancake batter. "Or bewildered, for that matter."

"You're doing great," Alex says, standing next to her.

When Hayley hands me my plate, a smiling pancake stares up at me. "This isn't resolute," I complain, which is how I woke.

"You're always smiling," Hayley answers. "So even if you are feeling resolute, or whatever, you still look happy to me."

The tennis court is hot. Hayley doesn't wear her tennis dress. Instead she has on a faded pair of surfing shorts, a turquoise blue tank top, and Converse low-tops, probably with black soles. As usual, Peter and Alex are dressed in cutoffs and bleach-stained T-shirts with stupid jokes. We've donned the baseball hats with mosquito netting—this time to keep blackflies and horseflies from landing on our faces.

Alex, Peter, and I didn't actually know one another until our final year of college: Peter started a year ahead of us, but took time out to hike the Appalachian Trail and "get straight with God," even though he didn't believe in God then, and still doesn't. Alex hung out with the crowd of people who had gone to high schools whose formal names started with definite pronouns, instead of no pronouns at all. They read primary sources in their high school history classes, and this made them intellectuals from the get-go. The rest of us, like me, had our epiphanic moments the first time we spoke the word *epiphany* in class instead of church.

"Should we play, or just play around?" Alex asks.

"Remember, I've only played three times," Hayley chimes in.

"Hit," Peter answers.

Peter and I pair up, hitting nice, even strokes to Hayley and Alex. The court is turf, not clay, so the ball moves slowly. This gives me enough time to remember to roll to the balls of my feet and crank back my racket.

"Nice," Peter says to me.

I'm no tennis player—just high school PE and games with friends. The first time Peter and I played tennis, he hit the ball to me with such perfection that I was able to return it hard and straight. Each time my racket kissed the ball, it made a satisfying sound, like a bottle of champagne being uncorked. Peter confessed he wanted me afterward, right there on the public tennis court underneath the Williamsburg Bridge.

The order switches. Peter hits to Hayley. "Watch the backspin," he says, even before his ball lands. "Move up."

Hayley swings but misses it completely, which I've done numerous times before. She doesn't say a word.

"Nice try," Alex says.

"Those are tricky," Peter says.

When Hayley tries to restart the rallying, she drops the ball, swings, and misses completely.

"Fuck," she says, throwing her racket on the ground and shuffling toward the gate.

"Don't worry," Alex calls. "It's a damn frustrating game."

"And it's hot," Peter says. "I'm on my edge."

They both head toward her. I spin my racket in my hand, twisting it, letting it go, then catching it by the grip. It's the sort of obsessive thing I did a lot when I was a kid. Like making self-improvement lists or trying to jump rope for an hour straight or memorizing poems. I throw the racket into the air, like a baton, and it twists several times. I miss, and it hits the turf with a thud, like the sound of a small animal meeting the tires of a car. Neither Peter nor Alex looks back at me.

Hayley vetoes croquet. In a rare show of controlling his competitive urges, Peter says he doesn't want to play cards—"not on a day as beautiful as this one." Because of the mosquitoes, spending the day in a hammock with a book is out of the question. Finally we agree on a swim in a small lake on the mainland. The road is narrow and twisty, like a ball of unraveled yarn. Alex takes the turns fast. Out the window, I see the place that Alex pointed out the last time we were here where a freak tornado touched down years ago and cleared a square mile of timber in less than thirty seconds.

"How fast can this do a hundred?" Hayley asks suddenly, leaning forward in the gap between the front seats, one elbow on Peter's headrest, the other on Alex's, her chin on her forearms.

"The Wagoneer?" Alex says. "No inkling."

"Could it even do a hundred?" Peter says.

"Oh, sure, it would do a hundred," Hayley says. "People race cars like this out at the track where Geoff drives, and they do a hundred, easy, without souped-up motors. I bet this could do it in ten seconds or so."

"Starting from a standstill," Alex asks. "Is that what you mean?"

"How fast it can accelerate?" Peter echoes.

"Yep," Hayley answers. "From zero to a hundred."

"Should we try it here?" Alex asks. "See how fast we can make this bad boy go? There's a straight stretch in a couple of miles."

Peter laughs. "This bad beast."

I try to catch Peter's eye in the rearview mirror, but Hayley's head is in the way. "Sounds stupid and dangerous."

"Geoff and I do it all the time," Hayley answers. "If we come on another car, we'll just slow down and try again."

With this, she's thrown down the gauntlet. There's no way Alex and Peter will miss the chance to prove they're just as cool as Geoff.

"I'm getting out," I announce. "Less weight," I add, an afterthought. I'm hoping Peter will offer to wait with me. *I'll keep Sylvie company. I'll let you two hotshots eat up the road.* But he doesn't, of course.

"Are you sure?" Peter asks, before they let me off on a gravel shoulder.

"Oh sure, I'm sure. Have a great time."

Peter certainly hears the fake cheerfulness in my voice, so

forced I almost choke on it. After the three of them peel out, I stand there, the tanginess of the evergreen trees that line the road mixing with the dullness of the dirt that I'm mindlessly kicking up with my toe. I'm mad at myself for not playing, even though it's a stupid game, stupid like so many games that people play.

I went to college with two body-size duffel bags and my bicycle taken apart and packed in a box. At the airport, ninety minutes away, I'd had to reassemble my bike curbside and ride Peter Pan for the last leg of the journey. The small New England town that was to be my home welcomed me with a downpour. I locked my bags to a signpost and took off on my bike, trying to figure out where I was supposed to go. All my neatly folded clothes, clothes my mother doubted would be in fashion "back East," were wet by the time I returned to ferry them to my new dorm room. At first, everyone thought my boots and Lees were quaint. "You grew up on an orchard?" boys would ask at parties, eyeing my leather belt. "Yep," I'd chirp and then launch into an explanation until it dawned on me that they weren't really interested in growing fruit trees. I saved the money I earned from working in the cafeteria and bought a pullover fleece and Doc Martens. I earned an A in my first lit course and spent my free time in my professors' office hours so that by the time I graduated, no one could see how ill at ease I sometimes felt. I could handle a hard frost that hits before the peach trees have shed their blossoms, but the rules that everyone else seemed to have effortlessly mastered—eating rice with chopsticks, or networking, or lining up the perfect internship—still seemed cryptic. Through sheer effort, I tried to hide my sense of being two moves behind. Even now, even after succeeding by the most conventional measures, this feeling lingers.

I hear the sound of the car before I see the Wagoneer. Hayley's at the wheel with Alex next to her. Peter's in the backseat. They're sitting up very straight and looking ahead. It's impossible to judge how fast they're going. As they come closer, they seem to go faster until they flash by—a streak of forest green. Then, as my perspective changes, the car seems to slow down. I hope Hayley's wrong about a hundred without a souped-up motor.

Before I know it, they're back, the car spraying gravel on the shoulder.

"How'd it go?" I ask.

Hayley leans across the seat. Her chest is touching Alex's shoulder, and she's grinning. The dimple in her left cheek is as round and perfect as a small pie cherry. "Twelve-point-three seconds," she answers. "A little slow, but not too bad. This thing probably just needs a tune-up and a couple quarts of high-performance oil."

"It was great," Alex says, grinning. "I think I've gone a hundred before, but never like that." He gives Hayley a playful punch on the shoulder. "You've whetted my appetite for speed."

"Fantastic," Hayley says to him. "You'll see. Going really fast gives you such a rush, about ten times more intense than this."

Peter rolls down his window: "The rush I had was already pretty intense."

"Are we going to the lake now?" I ask.

"Not yet," Hayley says. "There's another thing we want to do. It's really cool. It's kind of like a game of trust. Two people sit in the driver's seat—one person between the other person's legs. One person drives while the other directs."

"I don't get it," I say.

"The person who's driving can't see," Hayley explains. "Either the driver is blindfolded, or the other person covers the driver's eyes."

"What?" I ask.

"The other person, the person sitting behind the driver—Geoff and I call him the director—gives the blind driver directions," Hayley explains. "You know, like a little to the left, sharp turn to the right, slower, faster."

"That's crazy," I say.

"It sounds great," Alex says.

"I bet Sylvie doesn't want to do it," Peter says. "It's not her thing."

I glare at him: "You're right."

"Luckily that doesn't mean it's not my thing," Peter says. "Should we play rock, scissors, paper to see who goes first?"

"It's my idea," Hayley says, "so I get to drive. It's what gives me the biggest rush."

Alex groans when his scissors are crushed by Peter's rock. Peter's lame for letting his competitiveness get the best of him, for not giving Alex first dibs.

"Don't worry. You'll get your turn," Hayley says as she gets out of the driver's seat to let Peter in. Alex jumps out, and we watch the two of them arrange themselves, Hayley in the *V* of Peter's legs with Peter's chin just skimming the top of her head. It reminds me of when my dad used to let me sit in his lap and steer the truck down our gravel driveway when I was a child.

"This wouldn't work if you were taller than Peter," I say.

"No, it's really better if the driver's shorter than the director. When Geoff and I do it, I always drive."

Hayley grips the steering wheel, and Peter clamps a hand over each of her eyes. "No peeking," he says.

"Okay, Peter," Hayley says. "It's easy. You just tell me to go left or right, a little more or a lot. You'll also tell me when I need to slow down or speed up. For now, we'll stick to the basics: no U-turns, no passing other cars, or things like that."

She wiggles between Peter's legs. He flips up the sun visor, then replaces his hands over Hayley's eyes. "Comfy?" he asks.

"Yep," she answers. "And I can't see a thing."

"Okay, you're going to turn slightly to the left," Peter says. "You'll go up a little bump to get back on the road. Take it slow. There's nobody coming."

Those are the last words we hear before the Wagoneer goes rolling away from us. Alex looks longingly after them.

"This is crazy," I say.

He grins. "Hayley's so crazy. She's something else."

After looking both ways, I dash across the road and walk slowly in the direction Hayley and Peter have driven. Several cars speed by, bulldozing air toward me, blowing my clothes against my body. Each time this happens, I slow down and hug the shoulder a bit more. In the distance, I spot what I think is the green Wagoneer—the blind driver and the director—returning.

The car's about a half mile away when I step into the lane of oncoming traffic.

"What are you doing?" Alex calls. "Sylvie!"

The car comes toward me until I imagine I can see Peter, wrapped around Hayley, and Peter can see me, standing in their path. I don't move because I know Hayley wouldn't if she were in my position. Then I shut my eyes, just like Hayley, and wonder whether Peter will tell her, "Time to brake."

The low hum of the car grows louder. In the abstract, it's a beautiful sound, like nighthawks diving from a high eddy of air for insects far below, but in practical terms, it means the car is coming closer. I know how little resistance my body offers, how easily I will be thrown into the air, how quickly I will drop. "Sylvie!" Alex shouts. "Jesus Christ, Sylvie!"

Then something shrieks, and the air fills with the acrid smell of burning rubber. I open my eyes; the car is about ten feet in front of me. The door jerks open, and Hayley falls out of the car and onto the pavement. She rises, brushing off her hands. "What the fuck, Peter? Why didn't you tell me to stop?"

Peter says something that I can't hear, or at least I think he does because Hayley takes a step toward the car and yells some more: "What? That's no excuse."

He gets out. "I was going to," he insists. "There was still space." He reaches for her. "Are you okay?"

Hayley snatches her hand away from him. "I cheated. I peeked. I felt your fucking body tense, and I waited for you to give me something, you know, like 'Stop. Sylvie's in the middle of the road,' and I waited, and Jesus Christ, you just sat there saying nothing."

She kicks the front tire, hard. "What the fuck? What the fuck is wrong with you?"

Peter stands there, his hands at his sides like useless things. Alex is still on the shoulder. The only person who moves is Hayley. She strides toward me, taking purposeful steps. I expect her to begin screaming, but she doesn't. A car approaches from the opposite direction, slows down, and from the window, a man calls out, "Everything all right there?" Hayley hugs me, and I wonder how the man must see us, the four of us standing in a constellation around the car in the road, how differently he must see us from the way we see ourselves, how differently I see Hayley and even myself since she stopped the car. She is squeezing me so tight, I can feel her heart hammering against my chest, and for the first time in what seems like ages, I feel my own.

MEMO

To: Philip
Fr: Anna
Dt: July 12, 2011
Re: Why We Didn't

Purpose

The purpose of this memo is to—

Never mind.

You know, by now, that the memo is a form I like, one that

we often use in my business for thinking through the hierarchy of effect (how to move consumers from awareness of a product to the conviction to buy it). A disclaimer: I am not trying to sell you anything. I am not even trying to sell you my version of the truth. I know you will find holes in my argument, illogical conclusions—we may even disagree upon the facts. My mind is far from your brief-drafting machine, a brain capable of producing meticulous legal arguments just as soon as you've sucked down your morning coffee. I know, I know: it doesn't come easy, and such assumption-making about your intelligence and all your accomplishments is unfair. I've learned (not without practice, correction, nagging, even machine-gun bursts of impatience) that the last thing you want to hear is "You're so brilliant and accomplished, et cetera, et cetera, I know you'll get it done." Instead, as instructed, I have tried my best to say the following:

I hear that you are stressed out, and I hear that things are very difficult for you right now. If there's anything I can do to help, please let me know.

But sorry. Back to the matter at hand.

Data Method Assumptions

I wish interpretation were as easy as

If $x = 3$, and $x + y = 10$, then what is y equal to?

Ergo: If we were having so many conflicts over things large (whether to have one child or two, buy a bigger place, invite your best friend to our wedding, given your shared history) and small (organic versus nonorganic produce, the amount of meat in our diet, the best bicycle route back and forth to the park, allocation of bookshelf space in the living room, and so on), then the bickering and long, hurt silences would not likely diminish after we tied the knot. But future happiness is tricky to predict, especially when your married and partnered friends are counseling that hard work equals long and happy unions while also narrating half-funny, half really fucking seriously alarming stories whereby wedding planning and wedding ceremonies are likened to haunted houses filled with hidden demons and people who give fright merely because you didn't expect them to appear.

Let's face it: you and me, Phil, we were hard workers. We'd swallowed that most hallowed American value hook, line, and bait. So much misplaced ambition, so much longing for intimate recognition. We wanted what almost everyone thinks they want: to fall in love and live happily ever after.

Time Line

February 2009	Met at the party of a friend of a friend, began e-flirtation.
March 2009	Ceased for murky reasons.[1]
May 2009	Resumed, presumably after period of mourning ex had ended.

1 I said, "Let's meet in the real world." You said, "I'm unfit for female companionship."

June 2009 Had first date. Discovered mutual love of dirty martinis; lap swimming; little precious objects known as clutter to most, but not us; making lists of fun things to do.

July 2009–April 2010 Enlarged carbon footprint; earned free tickets; gained intimate knowledge of tarmac.

October 17, 2009 "Will . . .?" "Yes!" "How much money . . . ?" "What!"

October 17, 2009 onward Engaged? Yes! Happy? Questionable.[2]

December 2009 ". . . open marriage?" "Shouldn't you have . . . ?"

April 2010 Mingled pots and pans, sheets and towels, my debt and your assets; changed voice mail message, living room furniture but agreed to leave last names untouched.[3]

---

2 You're the one who read me the opening of *Anna Karenina:* "Happy families are all alike. Every unhappy family is unhappy in its own way." Our first line: "Every anxious couple is anxious in their own way."

3 I know we're too old and established to hyphenate.

June 14, 2010 Bid adieu to catering deposit, said awkward hellos to dozens of friends over forty-eight hours: "Just postponing . . ." "Working out . . ." "Some issues . . ."

July 10, 2010 Didn't say, "I don't," but didn't say, "I do" either. You entertained overseas friends who couldn't change tickets without massive penalties while I weekended in the Hamptons with college roommate who didn't mention "postponed" wedding.

June 2010–December 2010 Scuffled on. Spent large percentage of disposable income sitting at an uncomfortable distance from each other on tan leather sofa. Learned to say, "I hear you saying . . ."

Discussion/Background

August 2009

We were in New York, and you wanted to see a show of male nudes at the kind of midtown gallery where no one speaks above a whisper. This seemed like a strange choice—we'd only been dating for two months, were still working out the kinks of our own erotic life—and there we were, our shoulders brushing as we looked at naked men lying like logs stretched across roaring streams and naked men making coffee (the ruffled apron a nice touch) and naked men against black backgrounds staring defiantly at the camera, naked men whose nakedness was not the point, and naked men who were decidedly supposed to be naked.

I did know at this point that you were sort of fascinated with nudity, because on our second or third date you'd sat me down at your computer and showed me a video of a shadowy figure dancing and singing haunting songs—sometimes more of the body was visible, sometimes less, but it was still clearly naked.

"Is that you?" I blushed as more of you came into sight. Your hands hovered above my shoulders like moths.

"Yes," you answered in your very serious way.

I stayed over for the first time that night but slept in the living room. You said you weren't ready for sex, but we could share a bed, and I said, "Let's wait. Waiting is more exciting." Lying on the couch, I imagined you tossing and turning two floors above me, a prince driven senseless by a pea buried under his tower of mattresses.

At the gallery your gaze lingered on a young man who'd just tumbled out of bed, who looked like he was ready for a stack of pancakes. "How does this make you feel?" you asked.

"Weird." There it is—that terribly vague word that, nevertheless, seems to describe so much of our relationship.

"Does it turn you on?"

"Not really," I answered.

We walked on to Saks, where you began taking pictures of mannequins. This was another one of your projects when we first met—out-of-focus photographs that made the human form disappear into an abstract arrangement of colors. Though you made your living as a lawyer, you were an exceptionally talented photographer. That's when I asked you: "Is this what you and your last girlfriend did?" The whole morning had been so odd, I felt like an understudy who'd stepped into another woman's lead. You closed your eyes. This was your tendency when you were thinking. By the end, this habit could whirl me into a tornado of irritation and even shouting. You hated this—you called me violent—but we weren't there yet. I still had the patience of an average person. Standing on the busy sidewalk, your camera cradled in your hands, your eyes closed. Your pauses—God, I'd always be imagining the worst—they could go on and on. I'd meant my question to be playful—playful in a way that was also seeking reassurance, wondering, trying to establish a boundary, etc. I realize now this wasn't the most direct way to ask for what I needed. As you continued standing, I felt the flood of a caffeinated buzz, neither pleasant nor unpleasant, just jittery and sharp, and I started to imagine the worst.[4]

When your eyes finally opened, you spoke with great deliberation. "I don't know why you're asking me this question. I don't know what you want me to say. Does the fact that I've

---

[4] I've had enough therapy to see how fucked up I am. (I'm not sure therapy helps you as much as it highlights your flaws.) Why would I go out with people who screamed, "Stay away!"? Built-in emotional distance?

done these things with other women take away from doing them with you? Perhaps you're setting the bar too high?" I shrank back because what you said was both logical and far worse than I had anticipated. You added: "*You're* very special to me." Do you remember? This was the weekend you told me you loved me. And I said I loved you too.

Halloween 2009

Your friend, his name was Jawara, was having a costume party. It was his forty-fifth birthday, and though he was now a hotshot lawyer whipping around the partner track, you told me in confidence that he had once led a different life as a dancer in the Senegalese Ballet. It was amusing to see pinstripe-suited Jawara baring his beautiful chest, his costume a red grass skirt and matching cap crisscrossed with conch shells. He was usually so grave—and frankly boring when he rattled on about mergers—that it was difficult to imagine him doing anything as light as leaping. It was hard to remember that, yes, of course, he had a life in his body. Everyone does. Jawara was a good man when all was said and done, despite the fact that his Halloween party was probably the beginning of the end.

We brainstormed, trying to come up with birthday-worthy costumes, but it was actually fun. This was one of the things we did well together: *projects. Our projects,* as you affectionately called them. When we were apart, I read (and you reread) *The Works of John Locke,* and we had long, very important conversations over the phone about the state and the extent to which the state actually protects us. When we traveled around eastern Europe shortly after our engagement, we produced a travel journal (though in the sections you wrote, you never mentioned my name, which seemed strange—which was strange—it was always "we" or "I," but never "A" or "Anna"[5]). You taught me how to take photographs, and you lent me one of your cameras, a camera that was worth more than my pitiful stock portfolio. I still remember the day we wandered around your neighborhood, looking for the sun falling against a brick wall just so, or an interesting crack in the sidewalk, or a basement window framing a beautiful spider. Then we returned home, and we exchanged our best pictures and wrote poems about them. I loved our projects—your curiosity and also seriousness.

But anyway, back to Halloween: You suggested costumes that involved various states of undress, which I still found charming, given how buttoned-up you usually were, but I came up with the winning idea. We'd each go as our unconscious.[6]

Do you remember? The spandex bodysuits, our attempts to find the best way to transfer the text to fabric? I wound up using fabric paints and made a glorious, unintelligible mess of curves and flourishes—letters that looked more like dying

---

[5] "Shall we get you some dinner?" you used to say, not exactly the same thing, but evidence of some kind of self/other dilemma that I still don't understand and probably never will.

[6] A confession here: this was my crazy friend Sylvia's idea. She explained automatic writing, a practice developed by the surrealists, to spill thoughts across the page. "Whenever you get stuck," Sylvia told me, and I, in turn, told you, "just write, 'I am hot, I am hot,' until something else comes to mind." "Do you still think I'm hot?" I asked her. Her cheeks colored painfully. Sylvie and I once kissed, which I suppose I should also confess. She likes to pretend it didn't happen.

trails of fireworks or hieroglyphics than the alphabet. You used a black Sharpie marker, and instead of transcribing your automatic writing, which you judged uninteresting, you mostly used poetry you'd written years ago.[7] The joke was your unconscious was "stark and uncompromising." One thought began and another ended, each block of legible writing framed by plenty of white space. Across your groin (the bulge held snug by a dance belt), I dared you to write, "Your unconscious here," and you did.

I knew almost no one at the party, except for Jawara and his partner. There's nothing liberating about a costume party. Nada. If anything, it was harder to figure who I could talk to. The man dressed up like a box of cereal? Stale. The tennis pro? Stoned out of her mind. I stood near the samosas and deliberated over the different chutneys. Occasionally a person would drift over, ask me what I was, take a step back appraisingly, and then pronounce the bodysuit a work of art.

"It's impossible to read," a Pippi Longstocking remarked.

"Of course it is," I snapped. "It's the unconscious."

I was so anxious right after we got engaged. I'd wake up in the middle of the night, worrying about the possibility of letting you down in one nebulous way or another. I'd snap on the light, open my computer, and begin working through columns of numbers that represented my debt without understanding what I was trying to figure out. I'd worry I'd fucked too many

7 The superego instead of the unconscious?

people, that I'd used myself up.[8] When I tried to go back to sleep, the conversation I had with your mother would pop into my head: Why don't you give this ring a test drive?

We got engaged too soon. We'd only been dating four and a half months, and we didn't even live in the same city. My parents: "How exciting. You're starting a new phase of your life." Courtship in the age of cheap tickets and cell phones can be terribly old-fashioned, an arranged marriage you arrange yourself. We didn't know each other, not really. Take the ring. It hadn't occurred to you to propose with one, and it hadn't dawned on me that this would be important.[9] Your mother came to the rescue and magnanimously offered hers; that was the first time I met her—the weekend of the engagement ring ceremony. You recited a poem (Keats? Wordsworth?). Your mother cried. Your brother, whom I was also meeting for the first time, threw his arm around my shoulder and pulled me into an armpit hug. Your father said, "It's taken you a long time, Philip, but we're so pleased for you." I was as small and dumb as a stuffed bear.

Does the Halloween story have a dramatic ending? Something I saw you do that I have hoarded until this very moment?

---

[8] "Get over it," Sylvia said repeatedly. "This isn't the eighteenth century. You're experienced but hardly tarnished." Once she even took me by my shoulders and shook me.

[9] I'm sorry this got dragged into so many of our subsequent skirmishes. I know you've said your failure to think of a ring is evidence only of your nerdiness, but it was hard to keep this in mind as we hunted for a starter ring for you as carefully as a beachcomber pursues an agate. A starter ring. You'd never worn one before, and this would help you get used to it. We looked until you found the perfect one: silver and braided. I bought it for you.

Is there something you've been meaning to tell me? I doubt it. Nothing happened, except I felt abandoned. I'm a baby, I know. Petty. It didn't help when I found you among the boxers and pirates, call girls and heads of state (your friend Lydie made a pretty great Hillary Clinton) with Aranka, her hennaed hands and her loud, grating laugh, prostrating herself in front of you.

Does Aranka matter? I don't know. Everything matters, and nothing matters. That's the great truth of failed relationships, the narrative and the absence of narrative. Each time you tell the story, it makes less sense, the smooth arc disintegrating into a series of jagged peaks. As you stand on one of its precipices, you can no longer see the way forward. How did you traverse from one point to another? How did you make the journey safely?

Conclusion

This is where I'm supposed to synthesize the information I've presented and chart a course forward.

In conclusion, we didn't get married because I was afraid I didn't really know you.

But of course, it's not as easy as that. I'm sitting in a house overlooking the ocean, and I've just drunk several glasses of Chablis and read through what I've written. It has been six months since we separated, and a little over a year since we called off our wedding, and a year and a half since you broached the subject of an open marriage (not that you really wanted one, you just wanted to discuss the idea of it) and told me about your relationship with your best friend (a woman), and twenty months since you asked me to marry you. *Time heals wounds.* This is true, though something like *Time wears people out* seems more accurate. You can only step on the same nail so many times before you have to choose between mortally wounding yourself and walking away. It would be easy to say that we didn't get married because you cheated on me, but what's easy is not necessarily true. Besides which, you didn't cheat on me—since we'd only been dating a week or two when you flew to Texas to see your best friend.

Of course, I see my obvious attempts at wit, which are, I suppose, annoying in light of the subject matter. Laughing until you cry is surely quite different from crying until you laugh. You are probably doing neither. I don't blame you.

(All these paragraph breaks, all these crevasses.)

In conclusion, we didn't get married.

That I can say for sure.

Was it because I didn't know myself as well as I should have? Or perhaps it's that old cliché: I saw the person I'd become, or the person I'd stop being, if I stayed with you, and it frightened me.

The weekend of the art walk? Remember it. Red and white helium balloons rose from our front stoop, and friends and strangers wandered into our house and studied the self-portraits you'd spent the last six months obsessively taking, the last six months we were together. Everywhere I looked, I saw you: kneeling on the ground, with your ear cupped close to a yellow flower, staring thoughtfully into a cracked mirror, lying on a teeter-totter in nothing but your birthday suit, wearing a plastic shroud in an attempt to re-create another famous photo. There you were and there you were and there you were: a flesh-colored boulder in a field of rocks, a brown trunk in a grove of pale aspens, hairy legs beneath a table, a face half fractured in a puddle, a man against a red backdrop dancing to some music that I couldn't hear. You left to run an errand.[10] I was supposed to *hold down the fort.*

---

[10] While you were gone, I slipped into my Halloween costume, and I put techno on the stereo, mainly because you hate it, but also because it has a good fast beat, and I leapt down the stairs, surprising the quiet art appreciators who were studying the arch of your foot here and the curve of your lower back there, all the fine variations of gray, and I began dancing, shaking my arms and ass, spinning and dipping, strutting and folding, repeating motion and gesture until they took on their own grammar, until the subtext became text, until lowercase letters all turned to CAPS, AND THE CAPS THICKENED **INTO BOLD, AND EVERYTHING WAS FINALLY CLEAR, AND WHEN I FINALLY STOPPED**, EVERYONE WHO'D BEEN BRAVE ENOUGH TO STAY, ALONG WITH THOSE DRAwn by loud music and a glimpse through the open door of a woman dancing, said "yeah" and "cool" or nothing at all, just shook their heads in dismay or shock before wandering out.

I did this, Philip; I did this and other things that you have characterized as violent, and that I would characterize as hurtful and also disruptive, rebellious, immature, and selfish. I said I didn't want to get married months before we postponed the wedding, and I called your best friend and told her I knew about your trysts, and I walked out of your house when you disappointed me in one way or another. I picked fights, and when you closed your eyes or wandered silently through the rooms we were supposed to share and I felt myself growing smaller, I didn't know what more I could do.

That day, I danced until just before it was time for you to return home.

When you returned, everything appeared to be the same. You are everywhere, and everyone is looking at you, and I will never be anywhere or anything, except as a spectator or a spectacle, angry woman, or violent bitch.[11]

This is why I left. Why I disappeared for good.

11 My word, not yours.

LITTLE PORN STORY

The first time the Porn Star showed up at Maureen's house, he walked around, inspecting everything. He flipped through the books piled on her coffee table and randomly read aloud things she'd underlined. "From *The White Album* by Joan Didion," he said, clearing his throat as if he were about to deliver a monologue. "*I was no longer interested in whether the woman on the ledge outside the window on the sixteenth floor jumped or did not jump, or in why. I was interested only in the picture of her in my mind: her hair incandescent in the floodlights, her bare toes curled inward on the stone ledge."* He walked into her bedroom and opened the things on the dresser—a cedar jewelry box, a playing card holder from Russia where she kept copper and brass bracelets from Nepal, a cloisonné ring box that held a small carved ivory elephant from Tanzania. Maureen was thirty, never married, well traveled. She had climbed Kilimanjaro, tracked silverback gorillas in Bwindi Impenetrable Forest, scuba dived in Thailand, dined on rats in Beijing.

He picked up two bracelets made from twisted wire and polished rocks and said, "These are ugly."

She snatched them: "No, they're not. I got them in Costa Rica during my junior year abroad."

He started to open the top drawer of the dresser, which contained a jumble of athletic socks, knee-highs, swimming goggles, Jockey for women, camisoles, silky bras, and chocolate-covered espresso beans.

"Stop," Maureen said. "That's private."

He went down the hall and into the bathroom. She listened for the door to shut so that she couldn't hear the click of the medicine cabinet opening and then the rattle of pill bottles being inspected. It would serve him right if he stole Kaopectate. But the door didn't shut, and instead she listened to his stream of urine splashing merrily into the toilet.

He came back into the living room and sat down next to her, so close she could smell the fake pine scent of his soap.

"You remind me of an ibex," he said. "I think it's ibex I saw last year when I was hiking up north."

Maureen wrinkled her nose. "Wrong continent. Maybe I remind you of a deer or an elk."

"No, that's not what I mean," he said. "I mean an ibex. I think that's what they were. You're skittish like an ibex."

Maureen made a mental note of *skittish* and tried to keep a straight face.

"Well, they don't live here," she said. "They live in Africa or Asia."

"Whatever," the Porn Star said with a degree of indifference that appalled her. Then he leaned close and started kissing her.

She was surprised, but she liked it. He kissed well. That was something that you could never know in advance, whether someone's lips would have the right amount of give, whether they'd be wet enough or too wet, whether you'd be dealing with a bossy tongue or hungry teeth.

The Porn Star knew how to do it all right in his own way, and she didn't mind—in fact it thrilled her—when he moved her hands underneath his sweater and said, "If there's one thing you gotta learn, it's that the hands go under the shirt." Then he pushed up her shirt, shoved a hand under her bra, and twisted her nipple as if he were taking the cap off a tube of toothpaste.

"Ow!" Maureen screamed, though mostly not in pain. She had no idea what would happen next, and this secretly excited her. "Look, let's get back to this issue of the antelope. Why don't we check the dictionary?"

"Shut the fuck up," he said, "and relax."

"Mon dieu," she said. "What a brute. I never suspected."

"You like a brute," he said. He took a couple of breaths.

"Well," he said. He breathed again.

Then she realized what the pauses had been about. Not excitement, not that at all. He'd been focusing on the logistics of freeing his penis from his pants. Sprung, he turned his attention back to her.

"Like it?" he said, beginning to masturbate.

The man with the dick in his hand. It reminded Maureen of taramasalata on spinach ciabatta, her favorite kind of sandwich in her final year of Oxford, when she'd loosened up and become a pescetarian. The incidental poetry of life! You're kissing a guy you barely know and he takes his cock for a walk. She was scared but also amused.

My little Porn Star, she thought, kissing him.

My Little Pony.

My Little Porn Story.

But this wasn't her little Porn Story.

The Porn Star pushed her back, pinning her on the sofa cushions. "Suck my nipple," he instructed.

She found it in his hairy chest and gently bit down.

"That's right," he said.

What a lark! To see his private parts!

"Look at it," he said.

"Touch it," he said.

"Yeah, that's right," he said.

This is what happens when there's a man with his dick in his hand sitting on your good living room couch, the one you've forbidden yourself to eat on, and you're being put through the drills. You alternate between fear *(There's a strange man with his dick in his hand!)* and curiosity *(The man is taking his cock for a walk! Where is he going? Where has he been?).* You also think the whole thing is a bit absurd *(Taramasalata on spinach ciabatta!).*

The Porn Star started to push Maureen's head down to his crotch. She said no, but he continued putting pressure on the back of her neck. She said no, no, no. No! It wasn't that she hadn't done this and that she wouldn't at some point in the future, but she first needed a reading on him. He stopped, and this allowed her to veer from fear back toward curiosity, observing them in a detached way: that man with his jeans bandaged around his hairy thighs and that woman with a roll of fat squeezed over the waistband of her pants. Maureen made a mental note to remind herself that everyone looks fatter in the presence of someone else. She saw them wrestling. She heard him speak. "I need you to suck my nipple. Yeah, that's right." The woman's hair was yanked, and she rubbed the side of her nose, a nervous tic. She observed her twist the man's hair around her index finger and tug. She wanted to discuss with this woman her earlier prejudice against hirsute men. What a funny word: *hirsute;* suit of hair. Waiting for the next scene, she watched.

The Porn Star had picked up Maureen in the mall before Christmas. He and the Bambino had been waiting in a line that coiled tightly behind the elves' cabin for a short interview and photo op with Saint Nick. Only $10, the sign said, Make your children's dreams come true. The Bambino looked like any other kid. She was wearing a red miniskirt and purple tights and clutching the Porn Star's hand. Occasionally she hopped, hopped, hopped on one leg, then triple-stuttered on the other, like the thought of sitting on Santa's soft lap sent a shock of excitement through her small body. In fact, all the kids vibrated as if they were screwed into an electric current originating in the elves' cabin. The only thing that messed up the effect were the parents, motionless lumps of shopping bags, winter coats, extra eggnog pounds, and worries about how it would all get done. Maureen didn't envy them, or the Porn Star, for that matter, though she could tell there was something different about him. He wasn't wearing a heavy winter coat, just a brown wool shirt, and when the Bambino hopped, the Porn Star matched it with a simple jig. When the little girl said something, the Porn Star knelt down beside her to listen.

Maureen was staring at him when he looked up. She smiled. He smiled. Then she hurried on to Sears to buy towels. In the middle of the bath and bedding section, she turned around, and there he was with the Bambino in tow.

"Lunch?" he asked.

"Lunch," he pressed.

They settled on coffee, which was lucky because the pauses had begun to exceed the audible exchanges by the time Maureen finished her small latte. The Porn Star and the Bambino shared a large orange juice over ice. In the midst of a lull, the Porn Star told the Bambino not to sulk.

"The Bambino's upset because we lost our place in the Santa line," he said.

"That's terrible," Maureen said to the little girl.

"My real name's Bambi," the Bambino blurted out. "But Daddy doesn't like it."

"Sweetheart, that's not true. But you deserve better."

To Maureen he said, "My ex," and shook his head.

When the Porn Star asked Maureen for her number, she gave it to him. Why not? Six months passed before she heard from him.

"Who?" Maureen had asked.

He mentioned the Bambino to jog her memory.

"Oh, right," she said.

They made plans to meet for drinks.

The second time the Porn Star came by her house, three days after his first visit, it was after ten, and Maureen was winding down, picking dead leaves off the potted tree in the kitchen, making a mental list of everything she had to do the next day: take the cat to the vet, return library books, make an engagement square, cook ratatouille. She would not finish everything. In fact, she knew she wouldn't start making the square for her friend's engagement quilt either tomorrow or over the weekend, even though she was supposed to have mailed it off a week ago. What a terrible idea, she thought, expecting us to want to make squares for a quilt. Who had the time? The effects of marriage on her friends were curious.

Who would have known that Lila, a bond trader who could best any man at dirty-joke telling, would want an engagement quilt and a white dress with a veil and train from Vera Wang? At their weddings, Maureen studied the faces of her friends for signs—of what, she was not certain. Perhaps she wanted some evidence that their bodies had been temporarily inhabited by aliens from the planet of Beautiful Brides (where every girl dreamed of being a fairy princess). Perhaps she was looking for signs of realism—vows in which the couple declared they bonded over "ordering takeout and reading the Sunday paper on Saturday nights, having cheerful sex a couple of times a week, and gardening." Her beliefs in the artificiality of it all were vindicated when a friend from work confided that she planned to carry a ten-pound weight in her bouquet. "I want my arms to look really cut," she explained. If Maureen ever married, which was about as likely as terrorists targeting forty-something spinsters, she would most definitely not have a wedding. No, she'd take the bus to the courthouse, or whichever branch of the government was charged with bestowing marriage licenses (aka tax breaks) and pay for hers in pennies. Afterward, she and her wimpy but intellectually beefy husband would go out for a fancy vegetarian meal.

The sound of the knock startled Maureen. The Porn Star was standing at the front door, wearing a knit ski mask.

"Who's that?" she asked through the door. She was scared at first, but then she closed her eyes and chanted her mantra: *Be brave. Be brave. Be brave.* Her whole life, she'd been working at willing away fear. She thought this was what strong women did.

"Who do you think it is?" he answered.

Maureen recognized his voice, even though it was muffled by the mask. And then she recognized his shoes, white with faded red trimming and stripes. "Unmask yourself, man, and then I'll think about letting you enter." Her first laugh was forced, but then the lightness caught, and her face relaxed, and laughing was as effortless as breathing.

The Porn Star peeled back the stocking cap and grinned. Maureen noticed again that he had strong white teeth. A line from a fairy tale popped into her head: "The better to eat you with, my dear. And with that . . ." She pushed it out of her mind. The Porn Star had been raised Mormon, his teeth protected from stain-causing substances like coffee and nicotine by church law. She opened the door. "What's with the mask?"

"Don't know," he said. "Just had it in the back of the truck."

The third time, he showed up at midnight. By then the situation had moved from curious *(Oh, how silly, there's his willy!)* to strange *(From planet Venus comes his penis)*.

"You could do this at home, you know," Maureen told the Porn Star. "Rent a movie or something."

He looked hurt. "I don't like movies that much."

"Do you really think this is a turn-on for me?"

"Kiss me," he said.

"Tell me how to touch you," he whispered.

"You have five minutes," she answered. "At 12:43, you must leave."

She was balanced on her hands and knees above him. His

foot snaked around her thigh and tightened to flip her over. He brought her hand to his lips, licking her palm.

"Hmm," she murmured.

His mouth found each of her fingers and sucked. She let the room fade—maybe she even fell asleep for a few moments—but when she woke up, the Porn Star was closing her spit-slickened hand around his penis. That was all he ever wanted her to do.

"No, no, no," Maureen shouted and began pulling up his white briefs. "No."

"Wait a sec," he huffed. "Just a little . . ."

"Get a trench coat. Hide in dark alleys. But please pull those up. I'm sick of looking at it."

Maureen turned it into a funny story for her friends. This is what women did: put an amusing spin on situations that were almost terrible. It was admittedly a weird sort of bravado, but she had her friends in stitches, repeating the things he said:

This here's my hat. It's for keeping my noggin dry.

You're a filly chomping to get out of the gates.

You turn me on because you make me talk smart.

"I don't know," said her friend Sylvia after Maureen noted the word *consummate* was enough to make the Porn Star whip out his dick.

"That's the punch line," Maureen groaned. "Your cue to start laughing." That they'd become friends was mildly shocking. Sylvia had stolen Maureen's grad-school boyfriend, but they'd bumped into each other at the same old boyfriend's wedding and bonded at the after-after party, where they both got a little weepy (well, mostly Sylvia; Maureen didn't do tears) about seeing Todd jisming with joy over a woman. They compared notes on his sexual performance to cheer themselves up. (Both had been mildly disappointed, not by the equipment, mind you, but by the owner's inability to make good use of it.)

Now Sylvia said, "It sounds a little risky."

"What? You want me to play the damsel in distress?"

"I just want you to be safe," Sylvia protested.

"Is this why our mothers burned their bras?" Maureen asked. "To play it safe?"

Another friend counseled getting to know him better: "The poor Porn Star, or whatever his real name is. It sounds like he wants you to take him seriously. He doesn't have anyone smart to talk to."

"Please. Listen to what you're saying."

"No, I mean it. You should be nicer to him. Maybe you should have a salon. Weren't you one of the lucky few invited to Goldman's salons in Oxford? The Porn Star could talk about the complexities of unwittingly becoming a porn star. I can just hear it: 'Hello, my name is Jed. I mean my name was Jed until I met Maureen. Now I'm not sure who I am.'"

"N-O," Maureen said. "Besides, he has a girlfriend."

"Oh, he does?" the friend asked, her voice becoming nasally. "In that case, you should be nice to yourself and get rid of him. Unless, of course, he's great in bed."

"Haven't found out." Maureen started to laugh.

"Nice snort," the friend said. "You're screwing around but not screwing?"

"This is coitus in the age of simulation, postindustrial intercourse," she explained. "Sex without sex. Bodies only touching at three points: my mouth on his nipple, his knee between my legs, my hand on his penis, but usually just for a couple of seconds. Or, alternatively, his mouth on my nipple, my hand at the nape of his neck, his hand on my butt."

"Less messy," the friend offered.

"Less everything," Maureen answered. "Less of less."

Two weeks after the Porn Star's first visit, the two of them sat in Maureen's backyard drinking gin and tonics. It was either very civilized, or Maureen was trying hard to salvage her self-respect. Everything was in bloom—the lilacs, the crab apple tree, the dandelions, and the yellow and purple crocuses—and the grass was still damp from the sprinklers. The Porn Star was wearing khakis with crisp creases running down the front and back, a nice brown belt, and a white dress shirt with the cuffs rolled up, revealing his thick, sturdy forearms. It was the beginning of the weekend, and Maureen felt happy. She thought that perhaps she and the Porn Star could become the kind of friends who sat in her backyard from time to time, the ice cubes rattling in their cocktail glasses. She imagined laughing over how they'd met, and someday even telling him the story of his nickname. I will try to be nicer, she thought, which was a funny thing to tell herself. I will stop playing games. She made a mental note that the Porn Star's name was Jed Caraway. She looked at him. He had reached the age at which wrinkles formed in the corners of his eyes when he smiled. She handed him a red and green cocktail napkin left over from Christmas. He took a piece of bruschetta from the blue plate.

Overhead, the sky was the same color as the plate. She wanted to point out the similarity to Jed. She wanted to show him that everything wasn't a pale imitation of the original. Instead she said to herself, "This blue is true," and petted the cat who was rubbing against her bare legs and against the metal legs of the lawn chair where she sat. The tomatoes were sweet; the olive oil, vinegar, and tomato juice had soaked into the center of the bread, but the crust was still crisp. The contrast created a nice texture. It was delicious, and Maureen hoped that Jed might comment, a kind of compliment-comment. But they sat quietly, chewing the bruschetta and sipping their gin and tonics.

Jed started to talk to her about erotic things, about the most erotic thing he'd ever seen. It was simple. A woman whose shirt was unbuttoned too low. She was kneeling down to retrieve a book from the bottom shelf at Barnes and Noble, and he came around the corner, in search of a how-to guide on electrical wiring, and saw down her shirt, a peekaboo of flesh and satin. Surprise is sexy, he said. Less is more. He winked and asked Maureen about her most erotic moment.

Well, she started, it was the summer after she graduated. "I was on a road trip with friends. That part doesn't matter, I guess. Anyway, I was at a gas station, and there were two guys there; they had the hood of the car up, fixing it. One of them was wearing jeans and a jeans jacket with nothing underneath. He looked at me, and for some reason, I didn't look away, which was what I normally did when I was in college, when I used to be embarrassed to look too closely at strange men. I kept staring at him, and he stared back at me and slowly slid open his jacket, exposing his bare chest for me to see."

Maureen paused, thinking about why she'd been afraid to look at men, how she had once believed that looking could invite something unwanted.

She continued: "I think it was strange because he was performing for me. That doesn't happen often. Mostly, it's the other way around—the woman performing for the man."

When she looked up, she saw that Jed was masturbating again. His hand moved deliberately up and down his penis. This was Friday afternoon. This was early summer in Maureen's backyard, and she was trying to have a conversation with him.

"That was a sexy story," the Porn Star said, smiling. "It got me turned on."

She picked up the plate and dropped it on the rock path from the house to the garage. "It was my story," she said. "We can be friends, but I'm not interested in continuing to have this weird sexual relationship with you."

"Weird sexual relationship?" He sounded surprised.

"Yes."

"Well, I'll have to meditate on that."

"Meditate, huh?"

"What's wrong?" he said.

Several weeks passed before Maureen saw him again. She was working on the quilt square, trying to think of something clever to commemorate Lila's engagement to Edu. For some reason, the only thing that came to mind was a silly nursery rhyme that she had known in elementary school:

Two little lovers sitting in a tree
K-I-S-S-I-N-G
First came love,
then came marriage,
Then came baby in a baby carriage!

Now, of course, that wasn't the order at all. After kissing and before love came sex. And after sex with no love came a liberation (or deadening?) of the emotions, a severing of sex from love, which Maureen had once declared a good thing, standing by this belief for many years. Sex was just an act. And after love, marriage didn't necessarily follow, though it could. Or marriage might precede love. Or it might exist independent of love. The two little lovers might climb down from their perch in the tree and find the baby already waiting in the carriage.

Maureen heard him knock, but by the time she got there, he had moved to the center of the front lawn. Through the half moon–shaped windows at the top of the door, she could see that he was facing her house. His sweats were pushed down and scrunched around his ankles; his white T-shirt fell to the top of his hips. His hand was on his penis. Maureen thought about going into the living room, opening the curtains, and sitting down on the couch to watch the whole show. She imagined the picture that would form in her mind—all the details that she'd missed before by being too connected, too close: the way he moved his hand and how he held his body, his hair, his expression, the color of his skin. She would simply focus on the image: the man on the lawn outside the window masturbating.

Maureen stood, thinking about whether she could do all of this, but she felt scared. She felt scared and sad, and finally disappointed that she couldn't will herself to walk into the living room with a funny rhyme already forming in her mind. In the kitchen, she called the police.

THIS IS JUST TO SAY

You know you have reached a certain age when you learn that your BFF (in today's vernacular) is writing a memoir. "It's nice to be writing on an advance," she notes. Of course you're happy for her, the girl who taught you how to shave your legs and introduced you to eyeliner, Emily Dickinson, and Ivy League colleges, your locker partner and confidante from seventh grade onward. You have long admired her intelligence, her beautiful sentences, the way she could hunker down in the hallway right before class and scribble out a perfect compare/contrast essay on *Heart of Darkness* and *Apocalypse Now*, the only two things you remember studying in AP English. You think about those lazy late afternoons on your sleeping porch with the smell of the flowering crab apple riding little eddies of air through the open windows and rainbows darting like schools of tropical fish across the walls as your crystal prisms twirled in the light. Dreamy! Your BFF propped herself up against your pillows underneath the glow-in-the-dark stars you'd arranged into several constellations when you were eight and obsessed with astronomy and the fuzzy pink bat you'd hung more recently, opened the leather-bound diary that you envied, and read her newest poems while you hmm-hmm-hmm-ed in a way you hoped conveyed profound admiration for her verse. "That's *soo* amazing," you said afterward, praying she wouldn't press you for specific reasons why. When she did, you searched for the right words to *obfuscate* (SAT prep) the truth: that you didn't understand them well enough to say anything meaningful.

You were never a poet. One of your poems, whose title was something like "Is This One Man's Fate?" was about a moth repeatedly drawn to a lightbulb until it singed to death. At a statewide creative writing camp for kids like you and your BFF, kids who mooned over words and socialized in study groups, the local bearded bard told you to stop trying so hard. You were showing him the masterpiece you'd suffered over for days about chained dogs and spiritually dead lawns and proud flags wilting like lettuce, a poem you'd written after wandering through *bad neighborhoods* for inspiration.

"This, for instance, is a very good poem," the bard said, pointing to a little ditty on a neighboring page:

I like coffee
I like eggs
I like soccer players' legs

You went red with shame, embarrassed by the idea of an adult being privy to feelings you weren't sure you had. You can't even remember if you had a crush on a particular soccer player, or if you'd just written the poem because you liked the sound of it. You do remember that your BFF made out with a super-gorgeous fullback from a rival high school. She was interested in boys long before you were, or maybe it was that boys were interested in her. The poet also touched upon one of your sensitive spots: trying hard. This was what you specialized in. You weren't a natural genius like your BFF or Roderick Netermyers, who in a single day whipped off a semester-long biology project on the effects of caffeine on athletic performance. (Never mind that he had to fake all his data.) At that time, you thought of yourself as *just* a hard worker, a plodder who *only* made good marks through sheer discipline. For your AP Bio project, for example, you cloned a carrot. This involved driving to the local university several times a week, where you wrestled your hands into plastic gloves and checked on the progress of your experiment under a sterilized hood. Mostly you had to monitor whether there were sufficient nutrients in your petri dish to feed your little orange nub. The nutrients? You can't for the life of you remember what the sticky gel consisted of—come to think of it, you're not sure why this experiment of yours was considered cloning and not just gardening.

For her experiment, your BFF did something far more exotic on pheromones. She was testing the theory that attraction is mostly chemical and not a conscious choice, not a careful tabulation of how cute so-and-so looks in his wire-rimmed specs and brown slouchy corduroys, how much you admire the way he dances to the Talking Heads, making subtle movements of his upper body while his feet remain firmly planted, how you melt at his old-fashioned greetings versus your misgivings about how frequently he wants to discuss *The Naked Ape*, specifically how often the typical male thinks about sex in an hour. Yuck, your seventeen-year-old self thought but never said aloud.

If you were going to write your own memoir, you would definitely include your BFF's experiment. She recruited couples and pairs of best friends as test subjects, and they agreed to wear cotton balls taped in their armpits for a whole day and forgo all the products they usually wore to mask their natural smell: Dial, Chanel, and ChapStick; Noxzema and their mom's Night of Olay. At the end of the day, everyone gathered to see whether they could correctly identify their partners. You can't recall whether couples fared better than friends, though you do seem to remember that your BFF failed to choose the damp, shriveled cotton ball saturated with your essence. Or perhaps you were the one who plucked up a cotton ball smelling of ambition and hunger and teacups of melancholy and immediately thrust it back to its designated spot, the bagel you ate for lunch rising dangerously fast. Your BFF was always on a diet and often moody. Were the two connected? You're not sure. Her moods scared you. You often felt responsible, or rather you thought if you did everything perfectly—if you were the nicest, most conscientious best friend ever—you might cheer her up. You tried to be punctual, say the right thing, agree or disagree gently. Ah, adolescent narcissism! Face it, though: you're still susceptible to this kind of magical thinking. Which is why you and your BFF don't spend much time together anymore. Which is why you haven't seen or talked to her in three years. Which is why it's probably better, or at least more honest, to call her your BFFY (Best Friend from Youth).

You're happy for her. Maybe you're a little jealous, but jealousy is natural. You have watched from afar as she fought her way to the top of her Ivy League class, aced the LSATs, edited the law school journal, was courted by a white-shoe firm with a reputation of making pulp of women. You knew she would do well because she is so brilliant and well connected and very good at making strategic decisions and willing to do whatever success requires. After she tells you about her memoir, you e-mail back:

Dear Rhadika,
Wow! I'm surprised. This is such a switch from the law,

but you're such a talented writer. I can't wait to get my hands on a copy. What's it about?

Love,
Tabitha

A day or two passes before her name appears in your Inbox. Her memoir, she writes, is about quitting the firm for a year (you had no idea she did!), surfing from California to South America, meeting the man who is now her husband (did they have a wedding?! Were you really not invited?!). It started as an essay about radical rebirth (it is hard to imagine your old friend hanging five or ten), but the poetry of bombs and barrels, the beauty of lining up beyond where the waves were breaking and looking out into the vast and always changing sea . . . "well, it was like nothing I'd ever done before, and I ended up writing a hundred pages of this thing in a fevered dream . . . Then I got an agent, and she shopped it around . . ."

You are genuinely happy for Rhadika. You are! You also recall your AP English teacher, the extraordinary Mrs. Pearlman, who wore high heels, showing you that poem by William Carlos Williams:

This is just to say

I have eaten
the plums
that were in
the icebox

and which
you were probably
saving for breakfast.

Forgive me
they were delicious
so sweet
and so cold

But never mind. Rhadika continues:

Sometimes in the middle of a long stretch of writing when I'm trying to explain something that happened in junior high, like why Christine Thompkins and I were mortal enemies, I'll stop and wonder: Is anyone going to care about this?

Junior high? How is junior high relevant to the year that Rhadika told her boss hasta luego and bought a longboard? What do thirteen, fourteen, and fifteen, those years that everyone tries to forget or at least excise from family albums, have to do with trading blue suits for board shorts?

Yikes! (You have not divested yourself of all your teenage speak.) She is writing about your shared past, and already—based upon the little information you've gleaned from her e-mail—you're convinced she's going to get it wrong. Take Christine Thompkins. She wasn't Rhadika's enemy, as far as you can remember. Indeed, if she was anyone's enemy, she was yours, not that you thought of her as such at the time, but she did beat you soundly in the race for seventh-grade president. God, what were you thinking when you took on Christine? You'd gone to the tiny feeder elementary instead of the big one in the foothills where the kids were already drinking and making out in sixth grade. You didn't have a pair of Levi's or an alligator shirt; you didn't have a boyfriend (Christine was already dating the most popular boy, who happened to be running for seventh-grade vice president); you didn't have straight hair or a membership at the country club; and most important, you weren't a cheerleader (Christine was). This, in fact, was the first of many poignant, misguided decisions you made: going out for seventh-grade cheerleader. At the tryouts, all the girls wore white shirts tucked into blue shorts (to match the school's colors), whereas you wore your favorite pink culottes and a polka-dot T-shirt and performed a cheer your aunt had done a million years ago as a teenager:

Go back / Go back into the woods
Because you haven't / 'cause you haven't got the goods
You ain't got the rhythm and you ain't got the jazz
And you ain't got the spirit that East Side has

It's not that you still wish your foray into cheerleading had a *Pretty in Pink* ending, though at the time, Molly Ringwald was your favorite actress, and the highest compliment someone could pay was to note the resemblance. You didn't quite play the part of the nerd in junior high and high school, though you definitely disappeared in the crowd scenes. Would the attention of a popular boy have changed this? Teenage self-perception is more ironclad than a battleship. You doubt a missile attack could have penetrated your insecurities. Besides which, actual attention from a real boy made you cringe. Take your secret admirer—the boy wonder who sleuthed out your locker combination (how he accomplished this still puzzles you) and began leaving little anonymous notes and drawings taped to the inside of your locker door:

I like to think of you
on days that begin
with mornings

His other missives? They've vanished from your memory, except for one that had something to do with wanting to be the pillow under your head. (Now, unfortunately, this reminds you of what Prince Charles said to Camilla about wanting to become a certain form of feminine hygiene.) Eventually your secret admirer called, announcing in a disguised voice (disguised how? You have no idea.) that he would unmask himself at the Christmas dance.

Junior high dances! Remember how you and your girlfriends circled up and danced with each other, pretending to have a riotous time while periodically stealing glances to see whether any guys were approaching. Remember how you towered over all the boys and slouched to make yourself shorter the handful of times you were asked to slow dance. Remember the first time a boy put his hands on your butt in ninth grade, and your body felt like a container you were spilling from. Afterward, you migrated in herds to the Copper Creek, where you and your friends, who never had enough money for pizza, ordered Cokes and 7UPs with extra ice and tried to spot your crushes but never ever talked to them.

For the big seventh-grade Christmas dance, your mom bought you a mushroom-shaped dress made from pastel pink parachute material from Jay Jacobs. It stands out in your memory because it was one of the few times your mom brought you a whole outfit, and you loved it. Your hair was cut in the asymmetrical style that was popular in the eighties (buzzed above one ear, big and poufy above the other), and Mom gave you the green light on baby blue eye shadow, pink lip gloss, and the small, dangly sombrero-hat earrings that your grandparents brought back from Mexico. (Anything besides studs required special permission.)

After spending most of the dance furtively checking out the popular guys with dark hair, intense eyes, and actual pectoral muscles (not that you noticed such things at the time, but these characteristics probably contributed to their popularity), growing jittery the few times their heads turned in your direction, your secret admirer appeared before one of the last slow dances, one of those aching power ballads. You immediately recognized him from the windowless basement art room, where you and your friends ate lunch to avoid the indecipherable hierarchy of the cafeteria. He had black hair, big glasses with brown frames. He wasn't a mystery. He was just like you.

"I'm your secret admirer, Calvin Hill," he said, his voice breaking. "May I have this dance?" He smiled and shoved his hands into his jeans before he seemed to realize that dancing would involve his hands and pulled them out again.

"Sure," you said. His tie was patterned with red and green Santa Clauses, and he smelled of shoe polish and peppermint. This was the first time you realized how much skill was involved in slow dancing—maintaining a safe distance from his torso while simultaneously keeping your hands hovering on the outer surface of his white button-down. Twice you stepped on his left foot. Once your knees buckled, and you nearly toppled over.

Afterward, did you hug or just shake hands? You try to call the moment to mind but fail. You hope you had the good manners to say thank you and good-bye, but you can't be sure. When your parents picked you up, the small of your back still felt damp from where he held you. What ever happened to Calvin Hill? After that night you have no more memory of him. Did his family move away? Did he start avoiding you?

Recently, though, you have been startled by the numerous blank spaces in your recollection of the past, you who once prided yourself on being able to rattle off every single thing you received for Christmas (even stocking stuffers like Hello Kitty erasers, plaid socks, and Jockey for girls) between the ages of eight and twelve. Case in point: that guy on Obama's White House staff who graduated the same year you did and even allegedly played for the boys' basketball team. You study his portrait in the *New York Times Magazine,* but you still draw a blank, can't visualize him in the pack of tall guys with big hands whom you adored. You fret: What else has gotten untethered from its moorings? How many memories of people and experiences, emotions and events drift like lost ships on the high seas because their lines have grown too old and frayed to hold on to?

Does Rhadika remember the guy whom no one remembers—an informal poll of your friends turns up nothing—the guy who has entered an orbit never even imagined by the popular kids—the football players, the cheerleaders, the soccer player who got into Stanford and then bragged that he'd probably have invitations from all the Ivies because he was that good with a ball, and subsequently got NEGed everywhere (remember how frighteningly thin those rejection letters were)? Probably the guy who is now Obama's right-hand man, and whose name you still can't bring to mind without Google, is not thinking, "Nah nah nah nah nah."

You'd like to talk to him and to Calvin Hill, and the soccer player, and all the other kids whom you passed wordlessly in the hallway. You'd like to know what those claustrophobic years were like for them. Back then, you divided the world into hardworking versus brilliant, smart versus intellectual, partier versus straight, good kids versus bad kids. Your categories were so fucking narrow! You joked with your friends, "These are the best years of our lives," as though everyone else was having a grand old time. It never occurred to you that the soccer player might have felt just as miserable as you did when Yale wrote,

"We regret to inform you . . ." Or that Calvin Hill might have spent the rest of junior high and high school feeling sorry for you. Maybe he could see how lonely you were: having a sweetheart at the tender age of thirteen might have helped you blossom. Or maybe breaking into your locker was just one episode in a series of gutsy things he did to woo other girls. It's also possible the whole incident has simply vanished, been buried beneath twenty years of more memorable experiences: seeing his college girlfriend's long black hair spread across a feather pillow, watching the sun burst out from a quilt of clouds on a backpacking trip through the River of No Return, standing to applaud his son's debut performance as Puck in *A Midsummer Night's Dream* . . .

Obama's right-hand man has probably forgotten you too.

You wonder what else you have misremembered or been too immersed in your own experience to see. The mother of a friend sends you photos from May Queen, your high school formal, and studying these three pictures—perhaps for the first time, you're not sure—it's hard to deny those weren't pretty good years, not the best, but not the worst either. The pictures make it look like a teen flick, with the boys in white tails and black tuxedos with red cummerbunds, except for one feathered-hair rebel who is dressed in Levi's and a blue sports coat, and girls in outfits ranging from puffy satin confections to floral dresses with drop waists. A girl whom you could never figure out because she was smart and quiet but also once suggested floating a picnic table down the river has on white saltwater sandals. You love that choice. Everyone is decorated: with sprays of white and pink flowers, buttonhole roses, a burst of yellow forsythia. Once again, you show verve and a grave misunderstanding of school fashion by wearing a peach-colored culottes romper and a wide white stretchy belt.

The shocking thing about seeing these photos is how little you remember of the evening: not the dinner at Ginny Simm's house, a friend who predated Rhadika, a friend whom you loved because she looked like Laura from *Little House on the Prairie* and once wrote a forty-five-page sequel to *Little Women;* not how this motley group of kids came to have dinner at Ginny's house, since by senior year you and Ginny had drifted into different social spheres. Heck, you don't even remember your date's first name, just his last, Leavitt, though you do recall asking ______ Leavitt to the dance (it was Sadie Hawkins style) and the machinations you had to go through to first disinvite another fellow who flirted shamelessly with you but clearly preferred another girl. The dance is also a blank—did you slow dance? If so, did you like it? You do have a shard of recollection that you and Leavitt hung out with his friends afterward. You know for sure that you didn't kiss, but you have a hunch that you came close, that there were some awkward moments when you were both aware of your bodies' proximities, where you both wondered what to do.

Is *not* kissing and telling as much a foul as kissing and telling?

Because Rhadika is in these photos you forward them to her. After several days, she e-mails back with some choice comments about late-eighties fashion—Rhadika is a very good writer even in the usually sloppy mode of e-mail. She adds: "I seem to recall we got really drunk that night."

Wait, what? You don't remember drinking that night. It is a point of old nerdy pride that you rarely drank in high school—once the summer before senior year with the boy from down the street (who will remain nameless) who sometimes goaded you, the Goody Two-Shoes, into doing slightly forbidden things like biking out to the airport after dark and crawling under the fence to watch the planes take off and land. That time, it was champagne, not an ideal first alcoholic beverage because it's easy to drink too much. Another time it was beer with the boys from the basketball team. You didn't really like the taste, but that didn't stop you from having a draft at the ACTU (the neon *C* and *S* were burned out) with a kid whom you kissed on the golf course in the rich part of town. Finally, there were the wine coolers you drank in the parking lot at the school-sponsored all-night graduation party, organized, you suppose, with the idea of keeping drinking to a minimum. (Dear Mom and Dad, if you're reading this, remember that I was pretty good most of the time.)

For the record, you're sure, or 85 percent sure, that you did not get *really drunk* after the May Queen dance with ______ Leavitt, whom you did not kiss, but maybe wanted to, and Rhadika and her date, who, you've heard via your mother, has become something of a Republican bigwig in local politics. (Ah, the deliciousness of liberal Rhadika attending May Queen with a budding Republican!) Either 85 or 80 percent sure, which is pretty sure. You begin to wonder what else Rhadika is writing about junior high and high school, all those years you faithfully shared a locker. Will she tell the world you were messy? (You were.) Will she remember how the two of you decided you were weird on the outside (because you wore men's V-neck sweaters backwards, the aforementioned culottes, and dresses fashioned out of dyed pillowcases) and she was weird on the inside (because she wore jeans and Izods with her collar popped but wrote strange, moving poems). Will she quote the words of your theme song by Tom Petty: "Hey! Don't come around here no more . . . I've given up. Stop! I've given up waiting any longer." Will she describe the legend of the purple jelly bean, the details of which you have forgotten? Will she recall what she did for you on your Sweet Sixteen—the vases of daffodils waiting for you in each classroom, so that by the end of the day you could not carry them all. Like love, they seemed boundless.

Will she also remember the fierce competition between the two of you? According to your adolescent accounting, she was naturally smart, and you worked very hard. She starred in school plays; you played power forward on the basketball team. She was student body secretary; you were History Club president. You took calculus, she took AP Physics. She applied to one Ivy League, you to another. Will all this jockeying for position figure into the chapters devoted to ages thirteen to eighteen? Scientists say that memories of bad things are more tenacious than those of good ones. Jealousy, insecurity, anger, fear—you can no longer remember all the reasons for the feelings—but these emotions never go away completely. This is why you will not be surprised if you learn that you are only a minor character in the section on her teenage years—or even, to find no trace of yourself at all.

DISQUISITION ON TEARS

A new noise captured my attention: the sound of someone driving a nail into sheet metal. I couldn't stop listening to it, and I couldn't stop shaking. Each time the nail was struck, vibrations moved from my head, down through my arms and legs, out the tips of my toes and fingers, and into the air. I glanced around the living room, expecting to see ordinary objects like the coffee table and the bookshelves and the fringed lampshade reflecting the way I felt, but everything seemed normal, except for the woman in the African batik, whose beaded headdress began to streak like tears down her head and neck. I closed my eyes, and the pounding continued for what seemed like hours until gradually the sound became gentler, and I realized that it was noon, and someone was knocking.

Very few people came to my door because my house was hidden. It was off the street, across a gravel lot, and through a gate that swelled in the heat and rain and would not budge unless you threw your weight against it. The path from the gate to the house was blocked by an overgrown pomegranate bush covered with rotting fruit that had been recently infested with small black bugs. When I left the fruit unpicked, I imagined flocks of dark birds covering the small bush and pecking at the dry husks. The person at my door had most likely walked underneath the pomegranate bush, oblivious to the threat of the bugs raining down—not that this had happened, but I imagined it happening. I had grown accustomed to always expecting the worst, except for the flock of birds, which would have been beautiful, like a handful of confetti suspended in the sky.

I eased myself up from the couch. My pants were damp. This was not unusual; the pain that pinned me to the couch was so intense that I often lost control of different things. It was as though my body still wept, even though I no longer cried.

Through the front window, I saw a woman without a head. I pressed my knuckles into my eyes, hoping that when the static cleared she would be gone, though I didn't count on it. In my experience, the universe was more apt to bring things than to take them away, and just as I expected, the woman remained. Her shoulders were like an empty table, an unexpected horizontal line. Her T-shirt wasn't crooked, even though she had no neck to anchor it. I squinted. In one hand, she cradled her head as if it were a baby, while with the other, she rapped steadily on the door. Suddenly she stopped knocking and lifted her head up to the screen and swiveled it back and forth, taking everything in.

"Hello," she said. "Anyone home?"

I screamed.

"Am I catching you at a bad time?" she asked, as if by screaming, I'd told her nothing more than that she was inconveniencing me. "I can come back . . ."

I tiptoed back to the couch, but behind me I heard the door opening. I screamed again.

"I can come back," the woman repeated, now standing in my living room in front of a poster of impressionistic pastel-colored sunbathers that my nurse had brought to cheer things up.

I turned and faced her. She was holding her head in both hands and nodding it up and down. A red cooler was at her feet. There was a chance I could escape; though I moved as if the ground shifted beneath me like choppy water, she would surely be slowed by having to navigate without her head in its normal place.

"If there's a better time . . ." She trailed off.

She was so polite that I started to feel inhospitable. And also curious. The truth was, I wanted her to go away. But I also wanted to know how she got by. She reminded me of a blind man I'd met who took photographs. He didn't even pretend he could see; he usually held his camera right under his chin or above his head. When the film was developed, he asked people to describe the pictures to him. "I had a sense," he'd say about every image. He photographed me eating lunch. I was having a bad year, but that day was especially bad because I couldn't stop thinking about the MRI I had scheduled for the following week, when I'd find out whether any new tumors had germinated in my skull. I was wearing a silk scarf instead of the long red wig that everyone admired, because it was very hot, the hottest week on record since the summer of 1927. The next day, the blind man appeared at my table, where I was trying to stay cool by sipping tea, and handed me a white envelope. "I have a sense that you're sad," he said. "But melancholia is exquisite." We talked for a while, and later we went to bed. Often, before I had an MRI, I'd wind up in bed with someone—sometimes a stranger, sometimes a friend around whom I'd been too shy—aroused by my fear that it could be my last intimate act. It was like breakup sex, my friends teased, except that it wasn't like that at all. The blind man played the flute beautifully, but as far as the sex went, he was clumsy and rough.

When I woke up after our lovemaking, he handed me a photograph: "Tell me what you see here," he said. The picture was bright and blank, as if he had pointed his camera at the sun or the surface of a lake. I had a terrible feeling that this was what the blind man saw, but that he couldn't put it into words since it was the only thing he'd ever seen. "Why are you leaving?" he inquired when he heard me snapping my shirt. "Not disturbing, is it?" It scared me to tell him that it was both dark and bright at the same time, nothing and something. I had enough problems of my own.

Meanwhile, of course, the woman was waiting.

"Why are you here?" I wanted to put on my wig before having a lengthy conversation with this stranger, but the Styrofoam head was bald. Then I remembered I was already wearing it. "Was I expecting you?" I said, twirling a strand of hair. Doing this soothed me.

"We had an appointment," she answered, shaking her head in an exasperated way. Her brow scrunched together, and she moved the head both up and down and sideways. It must have taken her a long time to master the gesture with her hands, instead of her neck. "I can check my calendar . . ."

"I believe you," I said, even though I didn't. I had a terrible premonition that she was peddling something, like knives, that her head was a prop that she would use in her sales routine. I imagined her pitch: "I'll cut off my head before your very eyes. Slides through gristle, clean as a whistle."

She sat down. It was strange to see the head lodged in the *V* of her legs and tilted back, looking both up and forward, as if it belonged to a body lying in a dentist's chair. "It's a cave in here."

"It's because you've been outside in the sun," I answered. "Your eyes will adjust."

"They won't, actually. My pupils don't dilate. It's a rare condition. Not that it's terribly severe, but it can be a nuisance. The worst part is that I can't see in the dark. In fact, I prefer light of the kind that today has brought us. Bright, glaring light. Then everything appears crystal clear."

"Can you see me?" I asked.

The woman tilted the head forward. "Say something again, please."

"I'm without hair." I had forgotten the word to describe myself.

"Bald?" She turned the head slightly so that it was more or less looking in my direction. "I can see the outline of you. But your features are blurry. Is there a reason you can't turn on a light or two? It would help me immensely."

My hands twisted into a knot in my lap. Before this woman's arrival, before my headache, I'd been trying to remember something about the type of car that I'd rented in Spain ten years ago. My friend Lilly and I had driven around Spain for over a month in the kind of car that didn't have a top. It was frustrating. I could remember the feeling of the wind in my hair, as if a giant hand were collecting it in a ponytail, and I could recall the smells, the hot brittleness of southern Spain and the heaviness of Barcelona, and I could see the straw-colored fields that ran to the edges of the walled towns. One of them boasted a Roman aqueduct built without a speck of mortar. I couldn't fathom how I could remember such an odd and unnecessary word like *aqueduct*, but it was lodged in my head, along with *ambivalent*, *catatonic*, *deracinate*, *contumacious*, *petard*, *noctilucent*, *leman*, *fillip*, and countless other words that I once memorized for standardized tests but never used in conversation. These words were like packing peanuts in my brain, burying the real goods (like the word for a car without a top) so deep that I'd never be able to pull them out. Each day, I seemed to spend more time up to my elbows in the box, senselessly grasping at anything I could touch.

I had thought about calling Lilly before my headache came and asking her about the car, but I had bothered her last week, phoning her up to find out the word to describe her and her sister, people who are born at the same time to the same mother: *twins,* she blurted out. She had to run but said she would call back soon. You could say I was a twin: me before the tumors, and me after. If you looked closely at pictures of her (minus the hair), the resemblance was there, especially in the eyes. Our personalities had diverged, though. She wore high, strappy heels and befriended people everywhere, even on the subway, while I padded around in ballet slippers that my mother gave me and worried that it was obvious when I wore diapers.

I reluctantly turned on a light. "Is that better?"

"Yes, now I can see."

"What business do we have?" I asked.

"You told me you wanted a disquisition on tears."

Here was another word I knew, *disquisition.* A perfectly useless word that was an obstacle to remembering the term for a car without a top. "Why did I want that?"

"You didn't say. You called and made an appointment. I've spent over three days doing the research. But if you're not feeling well, I understand, and we can make an appointment for another day."

I could tell the woman was lying. Her shoulders were

bunched together again, and the head in her lap was biting its lips.

"You're feeling uncomfortable?" she said. "If you're feeling the slightest bit uncomfortable, I can put on my head pack. Would that be easier for you?"

It was true. I didn't know where to look when she was speaking. My natural inclination was to focus on her shoulders, but her head wasn't there.

"Would it be inconvenient?"

"Not at all. Notatall," she said in a slightly more jaunty voice. "Usually I do put it on, but for some reason, I didn't this morning."

I suddenly wondered how she drove. Maybe mounted on the steering wheel was a giant head-size cup. "When did I call?" I had no recollection of calling her, but it was possible that I had called and forgotten. This happened with increasing frequency—conversations were being misfiled in my short-term memory, or disappearing completely, just as the birds would have vanished after lighting on the pomegranate tree and picking it clean.

The woman's body began to quiver and her eyes pinched closed, and she made incomprehensible sounds, something between hiccupping and singing. I felt alarmed.

"Are you all right?" I asked.

"The way you're dressed. That heavy coat on a hot day like this. Now that I can see, I couldn't help but notice. Oh."

The sound was giggling. She was laughing at me. She brought her hand to her mouth to muffle the sound. The gesture was so strange and small. The whole point of giggling into your hand was bringing it all the way from your lap to your mouth. "Oh," she snorted. It was true that I was wearing my winter parka, the hood trimmed with fur. I was often chilly, even on these hot days.

"And those," she said, pointing to my socks with toes like the fingers of mittens. The head began to redden and cough, showering her legs with saliva. When she pounded her chest, I could hardly stand it. "Oh dear me," she said, "Oh dear me. I think I may be choking." She spluttered on. "Would. You. Be. Kind. Enough. To. Get. Me . . ." While her torso shook, her head froze. Her eyes opened as wide as a mannequin, and her mouth twisted, as if someone playing a practical joke had put her lips on sideways.

I went to the kitchen for a glass of water. Moving made me realize that I had a rash like fine sandpaper on my butt from sitting in my wet underpants. I considered going into the bathroom to shed my damp clothes and apply talcum powder or a soothing cream, but I was afraid it would take too long. The bathroom was dizzying with all of its similarly shaped containers. I might accidentally slather toothpaste on my butt, in which case I'd have to scrub it off, thus aggravating the rash. Such mishaps had happened before. Once I had brushed my teeth with A+D ointment; another time, I had squirted nasal decongestant into my eyes. In another context, these mix-ups might have made amusing anecdotes, but in the context of my cancer, they weren't—at least not to others. I might laugh to death about them privately, but that was no fun.

I almost forgot about the woman, but then I saw the glass of water in my hand and returned to the living room.

The woman brought it to her mouth, like a blind person using memory rather than sight. Cupping her head right beneath the chin, she tilted the glass, dribbling tiny sips into her open lips. I glanced away; it was as if I were watching something very private, like a mother nursing a baby or a bald woman being fitted with a wig.

"Thank you," she said. "I haven't laughed that much in years. My lung capacity isn't what it used to be."

I looked at her in disbelief. "Leave, you headless freak."

"Tell me something I don't know." She giggled.

"You're a fright," I said. "There should be a law requiring you to wear a prosthetic device."

"And you're a fright too," she answered. "Sitting alone in your house day after day."

"I'm very sick," I said, surprised by how offended I felt. "It's difficult for me to leave."

"Why don't people take you out?"

"They do when they have time. But people are busy."

"Don't you have friends?"

I stopped to consider her question. It was true that I did have friends, but when I got sick and the tumors persisted against the doctors' aggressive attacks upon them, the friendships became difficult. I suspected that many of my friends thought I was going to die, and pretending that I was not going to die was a burden too heavy for them to carry. Even my roommate, Sylvie, had left me. It was also true that for a long time, I thought I was going to live. So shoot me. I was alive, and I thought I'd keep living. Also, I stopped calling them; it was so tiring trying to comfort them.

The phone rang.

"Aren't you going to get it?" the woman asked.

"No," I said.

"It's probably one of your friends," she said.

The phone continued to ring. I had gotten rid of my machine because the little red eye, staring at me without blinking, reminded me that I was always home. I didn't wish to abandon the idea that I might have been out doing fabulously fun things if only I had gotten the calls.

"I can't stand the ringing," she said. "How can you bear it?"

"Look," I said, "when I finally came to terms with the fact that I was going to die, many of my friends, who thought I was going to die much earlier, stopped being my friends. It sounds cruel, and at first I thought it was, but they were living, moving on, and I interfered with this."

"What about your other friends?" the woman asked.

"They're still my friends because they've always believed that I'll live," I said. "And when I was still optimistic, this suited me, but now their hopefulness fits me like old clothes."

The woman stood up and was heading toward the phone when it stopped. She sat back down. "No wonder you're by yourself."

"It was probably my father," I answered.

Her eyes lit up. For emphasis, she grabbed her head and moved it my direction, scrutinizing me. "Your father? Does he live in town?"

"Indonesia. He has a coconut grove." This was obviously a lie. My father had been dead for ten years. My mother lived across the country. After lengthy negotiations, she had agreed to allow me to live quietly in the house I inherited from my grandmother until I absolutely needed her. It was easier on both of us.

"Right," she said, clearly indicating that she didn't believe me. "Does he use a long bamboo pole to knock coconuts from the trees?"

She laughed. She was cradling her head in her hands again, rolling it back and forth like a basketball. Suddenly, I had a sick feeling that she was going to toss her head and expect me to catch it. Because my eye-hand coordination had been damaged with my third surgery, I knew I would miss it, and when I missed it, I didn't know whether her head would bounce like a basketball, explode like a ripe tomato, dent like a cheap aluminum pot, or get scrambled like the brain of a carelessly shaken baby.

And what would happen to her body if her head were lying on the floor? How would she find it?

I started to sniffle.

"Aha," the woman said as though she had caught me doing something naughty. "Over the phone you said that you no longer cried. But I knew you were lying."

My own head began to hurt again. I could feel the pain

pulsing like a sound wave from a small node buried in my front temporal lobe.

"Did you know," she said, "that crying is like urinating, shitting, or exhaling, that it cleanses the body of its waste and pain? Did you know that there is a difference in the chemical composition of tears that you shed when you're peeling an onion and those that spill when you're feeling sad, sorry for yourself, anxious? A study of ordinary men and women revealed that women weep five times as often as men, that the typical crying jag lasts six minutes, that people are most likely to cry in the evenings when they let down their guard, that there is no correlation between crying and age, except that babies younger than two months old do not shed tears, because their tears ducts are not fully formed. Were you aware of this? Were you aware of any of this?"

She lifted her head from her lap, her thumbs pressed into her ears, and offered it to me like a gift. But then I realized the gesture was a rhetorical flourish, an exclamation point at the end of her speech.

"Now," she continued, "I want to show you something."

She carefully placed her head back into the valley of her legs and opened the cooler. I wondered whether she was going to feed me. Offering food—casseroles, cold cuts, homemade cookies—was one of the few ways that people were comfortable expressing their care. I hoped she would.

She removed a small plastic container. Dip? I wondered. Perhaps she'd prepared crudités? I liked everything, except for celery, whose strings got tangled in my teeth.

"This is onion dip," she said.

I eagerly peeled back the lid, but was surprised to find nothing but an inch of colorless liquid.

"Onion tears," she repeated, and then I realized I had misheard her. "Smell them, and tell me what they remind you of."

"Nothing," I said, "except perhaps an old plastic margarine container."

She laughed. "And now smell this: brimming tears, most typical of the crying behavior of the human male."

I stuck my nose into the container. "These are familiar," I said, thinking for a moment. "They remind me of something from my childhood, the mixture of hot water and salt that my mother made me soak in when I'd hurt myself."

"Epsom salts," she said. "Exactly. And now this: cascading tears, a normal sign of women's pain and suffering."

The scent of the liquid was cloying, like the breath of a woman who kept her lips pressed together and rarely spoke. My visitor handed me another container: sobbing tears that smelled like a pot boiling over and bursting into flames. It was difficult for me to believe that all the containers fit into the small cooler, and that they held so many different types of tears: of willful toddlers, of irritation caused by small bugs and grains of sand, of yawns and sneezes, of fear, of silent weeping, of rage and disappointment, of crocodiles and other forms of fakery. She handed me container after container, and each one smelled like something that came to me in words that I found in my head and brought to the tip of my tongue without a thought. It was the first time in months I hadn't gotten terribly stuck in the middle of trying to remember something.

"I've saved the best for last," she said.

"We're at the end?" I asked, feeling a bit sad.

Her head deflated slightly, like a balloon with a slow leak, or the way faces look early in the morning before they've regained their shape.

"I'm afraid so," she answered. "Lacrima mortis."

The container was the size of a baby food jar, and there was barely a teaspoon of liquid in the bottom.

"This is rare, very difficult to collect."

I sniffed it gingerly. The liquid smelled of hospital, like brightly lit ammonia and anonymous starched sheets and uniforms, like the humiliation of the bedpan and the toilet bowl, like sapped blood, like an electric razor when it overheats, like bouquets with too much baby's breath and the distance between the sky and the window when you're not allowed outside, like greasy telephone receivers and plastic IV veins, like the staleness of the television playing for too long. The smell was so simple, so familiar, so disappointing. The pain got louder, and the container tipped, the drops of tears spilling across my lap as if I had wet myself again. I closed my eyes and concentrated. Someone was knocking somewhere, and I listened.

ANIMAL CRUELTY

Deirdre is not in denial about the mice. You can't ignore what you don't know about, and the mice took up residence in the cabin over the winter when storms pummeled the island, suddenly dimming the light of the afternoon, and no one was around except for the caretaker, who checked to see that the pipes hadn't burst during January's freeze. He wasn't paying attention, and the mice were small and had enough good sense to make themselves scarce as he trudged from room to room.

What Deirdre hasn't been able to face, but must, is that

she is pregnant. She must make a decision, or it will be made for her, and she hasn't told her boyfriend, Dale, and he hasn't noticed her condition, not because he is willfully obtuse, but rather because he is the sort of person who isn't especially observant, who wouldn't notice if she gained five pounds or developed a craving for mayonnaise or stopped having her period, who would never think of thumbing through her calendar or asking why she seems so distracted. She doesn't know what she is going to do, which is why she's spending ten days on a small, rocky island that can only be reached by prop plane or taxi boat, where there are no restaurants or stores—or people, for that matter, because it is early in the season.

She pauses at the front door. The sameness, stretching back to when she was a child, is what she likes about the cabin. Broken clamshells have always littered the flower bed at the base of the stairs, and her family has always hidden the key in plain sight behind an ugly macramé of nylon rope and sea glass. The main room, which she can picture before she steps inside, is filled with her grandparents' relics: a coffee table sliced from a massive ponderosa pine, shelves lined with A. A. Milne and cut jelly jars full of agates that her grandmother collected, lime green bar stools, lamps fashioned from driftwood. Even the water will smell and taste the same. This is why she has come.

Inside, of course, something is different. Change is inevitable; people just usually don't notice, though Deirdre does. First, it's the smell—not the cabin's usual scent of lemon furniture polish and burnt logs. It's the odor of sex and too much living, like a dark room in a cheap roadside motel where you're certain that people have hours earlier been doing dirty things, things you imagine but never do. The source remains a mystery until she sees a mouse dart from behind the couch, cross the wooden floor, and slip under the leather chair that was in her grandfather's house until he died. A mouse? She doesn't mind mice, but this is the first time in recent memory she has found them here. She shoves three T-bones into the turquoise refrigerator that matches the forty-year-old stove. While stowing crackers in the pantry, she discovers a yam haloed with mold and nearly throws up. Years ago, her father drafted a list of procedures for opening the cabin: turn on the water, flip the circuits, run the faucets, flush the toilets, build a fire. At the end of the typed list is an addition in her father's neat, blocklike penmanship: "Pour a drink." Deirdre skips to the fire, in hopes of restoring the cabin's usual smell, and then proceeds to a celebratory finger of whiskey. In the drawer that holds the jiggers and the silver stirrers, she finds a cozy nest of shredded cocktail napkins. She takes a big sip, pushing the amber liquid through her teeth, feeling her tongue go pleasantly numb. Then she flushes with guilt and dumps out the glass.

Evidence of the mouse invasion is everywhere: in every drawer she opens, every surface she touches, every dish she inspects. They have disemboweled one of her grandmother's needlepoint pillows and snuck into the silverware drawer and wedged black pellets between the prongs of forks. She sweeps the nooks and crannies and washes everything she can. She flips on the radio, tunes in the Canadian station, her favorite because she imagines they match the music selection to the weather reports. It is late afternoon, that time of day when people can feel worn out and old, and they are doing a set of the Rolling Stones.

Underneath the rotating water wand in the dishwasher is a shriveled mouse corpse. Deirdre can't imagine why mice would be drawn to the dishwasher, but there is much she doesn't understand about them. Dale is the one who, in recent years, has come to prefer animals to humans or at the very least sees little difference between the two. He is against using animals for research, having them as pets, putting them on display in zoos, and he has recently begun making outlandish statements, drawing comparisons between lactating women and cows, wondering in mixed company why there isn't human cheese. When he launches into one of these harangues, Deirdre tries to move out of earshot. After the mouse carcass crumbles in her improvised paper towel mitt, she stabs at it with the wand of the Hoover, another item that has been at the cabin since before she was born and should be replaced since its suction is gone. Defeated, she unloads the dishwasher and runs it empty, hoping the hot water will dissolve the mouse crumbs, the droppings, everything.

Kindness is a scarce resource. She appreciates this about Dale. But the human in her still sees mice as pests, little carriers of germs. She sets a trap, half hoping the mice will not recognize the feta as cheese, and places it underneath the sink. She eats dinner—salami, bread, two glasses of milk—standing at the counter. Then she goes into the children's room. Two sets of bunk beds snake along the walls like railway cars. The dresser is filled with games from her childhood—Mastermind, Blockhead, Battleship. She pulls herself up onto the top bunk, remembering how tall and scary it seemed when she was young, but now it seems less risky than the bottom, where mice might attack her in the middle of the night. The master bedroom is out of the question. Without Dale, the king-size bed would be too vast.

Almost no light comes through the heavy curtains. The clothes that Deirdre piled on the folding chair slump like a depressed man. "Dale?" she asks. She closes her eyes, hoping that when she opens them she'll recognize where she is. Something rustles outside her door, and she quickly remembers the wooden trap, the morsel of feta. Emerging from the dark cave of the room, she goes into the kitchen, which is flooded with pale early-morning light, and very tentatively opens the kitchen cabinet. There is a mouse, still very much alive, scrambling back and forth, trying to free its tail from the triggered wire. Deirdre can barely bring herself to look at the gray coat, the black beadlike eyes, the frantic movement of tiny legs and nose. She takes a step back, focusing instead on how the contents of the cabinet have been turned over and scattered in much the same way a tornado rearranges trees and cars, houses and bicycles. During the time she does nothing, the mouse sees an opportunity and makes a break for it, leaping out of the cabinet and racing across the floor, banging the trap behind it. Deirdre hesitates—she is not without fear of mice—before she grabs *The Nation* and attempts to herd the mouse into a paper grocery bag, but it outmaneuvers her, heading for the refrigerator, the trap scraping across the floor like sled runners over rocks. It suddenly stops, the wooden base of the trap wider than the space between the refrigerator and the wall. The mouse claws the floor furiously, though to Deirdre it sounds like nothing more than a handful of broom bristles, trying to find traction, trying to break free, and squeals.

The mouse is trapped, and the trap is trapped, and all she needs to do is bend down and pull back the metal wire to free the creature. His high-pitched cry is painful, and his movements are panicked. At one point, the mouse contorts his body as though he is trying to back up or do a U-turn, and Deirdre may be fortuitously free of the responsibility of doing anything. There is a clatter, and the mouse is gone, but the trap remains, and pinned between the wire and the wood is the mouse's tail, longer than her middle finger and healthy pink except for the bruised and bloodied stump where the mouse chewed it off. She flees the kitchen.

On the deck, she sits bundled up in clothes that other people have left behind and tries to distract herself by reading about gastropods in *Marine Life in the San Juan Islands,* about how the keen intelligence of the octopus allowed it to evolve and shed its shell. What about mice? Does losing a tail disrupt their balance, make them vulnerable to sneak attacks from behind, cause them to misjudge distance and get stuck in awkward spaces? Without a tail, will a mouse survive?

What would she be willing to sacrifice to stay alive? Her arm? Her eye? She wonders what she is willing to sacrifice for the baby-to-be, or the baby-who-might-be. Or for her relationship. The night before she left, Dale's reflection appeared inverted in the Steuben crystal cat in their living room. "Whatever you need to do," her upside-down boyfriend said to her, "you must do."

The thought of his generosity makes her vomit off the deck. Her stomach is tight and angry. The doctor says the nausea is good: the baby is settling in, taking hold. In a month, at the end of her first trimester, her queasiness should go away. In the kitchen, she rinses her mouth out with water before she sweeps the trap and the bloody mouse tail into a dustpan and throws them both over the railing of the deck. Then she calls Dale. She thinks she will tell him she is pregnant, and this is why she has gone away, though this is not the whole story. She doesn't understand the whole story, only that now that she is pregnant, she feels the need for certainty—not absolute certainty but enough.

"I thought we were incommunicado," he says bravely.

"Señor Avocado, how did you know it was me?"

"Señora Mango," he answers, "don't be a fruit case. We salsa together rather too well for me to have forgotten your juicy flesh so quickly. You haven't met a spicy jicama, have you?"

"Well, there is a yam here who is stripped to his starched underwear," she answers, sickened by how easily they banter even under difficult circumstances. They should know better.

"I'm getting jealous," Dale says.

"Don't be. He's rotten. I threw him away."

"So cruel."

Deirdre begins to cackle but can't keep up the game. "I'm sorry."

"Why?" Dale asks. "You can't help it. You needed some time to yourself."

She hates him for saying this, for being so reasonable. She should try to explain. What? She's not sure—that she is pregnant and this, along with a slow accumulation of other things, has made her question whether they should stay together. But doubt, fear, something—what is it?—keeps her quiet, makes her cowardly. She would like to punch herself in the stomach, but she can't. "There are mice. The cabin is overrun with them."

Dale snorts.

"They're driving me crazy," she continues. "I caught one this morning, but it gnawed off its tail and got away."

"You maimed a mouse." Dale sounds offended. "Great. Now he's dying slowly somewhere in the cabin."

She groans. "What am I supposed to do?"

"Just live with them."

"But they're small. They're always underfoot, or worse, they're not underfoot, and then I'm worrying about where they are, when they're going to surprise me."

"They sound just like children," Dale snorts.

This silences Deirdre. If Dale knew of her pregnancy, he would, she thinks, happily insist on having the baby, even though in the abstract he supports zero population growth and draconian quotas on births. He would behave gallantly, mustering a smile and proclaiming, "Rules are made to be broken," just as he'll eat vegetables cooked in butter when they are dinner guests of people unacquainted with his recent transformation from vegetarian to vegan.

"Just don't kill them," Dale pleads. "They haven't done anything to hurt you. Do the dishes and keep the food put away. Next time, we'll bring catch-and-release traps and figure out how they're getting in."

His plan is so reasonable. "I love you," she says.

He doesn't say anything back. Of course she loves him, though something has changed. She loves him from habit. She loves him because he is her boyfriend, and she has loved him for five years, and it is difficult to imagine a life that does not involve loving him.

"Be nice to the mice," he says.

"Okay," she says. "I guess I'll go."

"You go."

"I'm going."

"Okay, you're gone," he says, getting in the last word. This irks her.

She thinks about the moment she started to feel differently about Dale, how insignificant it was. They were on vacation, up here on vacation, and she was lying on the couch, reading the *Rough Guide to Australia* because she wanted to go diving on the Great Barrier Reef, and popping chunks of dried pineapple into her mouth. Her tongue hurt, her gums stung, but she couldn't stop herself from reaching for another piece of pineapple. And then Dale came in and said, "Wanna shoot some hoops?" And she agreed because she had to get away from the pineapple, and she'd read everything she could about the reef. What if the circumstances had been different? What if she'd been eating grapes and reading a mystery? She might have rolled her eyes at Dale's offer. Playing basketball wasn't her idea of fun. But they walked to the basketball court (where they also occasionally played tennis), and Dale taught her how to bend her knees, flick her wrist. "That's right, baby," he said, "it's all in the follow-through." She sunk that first three-point shot, and later she made a whopping three in a row and felt so giddy, so suddenly sure of her ability to learn all kinds of new things after telling herself for many years that she was the kind of person who liked knowing things, not learning them. After the ball's third swish, Dale jumped in the air, doing an impromptu cheer: "Two, four, six, eight! To whom do I masturbate?" He came down so hard on his ankle, it sounded like Velcro being ripped. If none of this had happened, if she'd just stayed put, maybe she would not have felt the unbearable weight of him on her arm as they walked together back to the cabin.

Of course this is not the real reason she wonders whether they should split up.

It is one among hundreds of reasons. People change in all kinds of small ways. What can she say? My boyfriend turned into an animal rights nut. He refuses to try new things. He's started exaggerating the seriousness of his hobbies. He's lost his edge. Each on its own is so petty, so insignificant. What's the point of saying anything?

For several days, Deirdre treats the mice like houseguests who have overstayed their welcome. When she finds a mouse in the deep tub in the master bedroom, she gets a bucket. Leaning against the porcelain side, she senses the limit of her stomach's give and imagines the thing inside her solidifying, forming opinions, mouthing, "Stop doing that." The mouse refuses the invitation of the yellow bucket tipped on its side.

"Little guy," she says in a voice she reserves for children. "You're a cute little guy, and I want to help you get out of there."

The mouse scampers to another corner of the tub, as if they are playing a lighthearted game of tag: he skitters away, she moves the bucket; she reasons with him, he ignores her. Her belly hurts—she is hungry or sick. "Get in!" she shouts, pressing the lip of the bucket into the corner, edging it under his body, trying not to do internal harm.

She drapes a towel over the bucket, not because she fears the mouse escaping, but because she is afraid of being infected with his panic. It doesn't work. As soon as she walks outside and into the trees, tiptoeing around the nettles and keeping an eye trained on the ground for slugs, she starts to worry about separating the mouse from his mouse friends, about his nest-building and foraging-for-food skills. She thinks of the raccoons wearing their bandit masks ambushing the mouse. She peeks down at him. He is already vibrating like an old-fashioned alarm clock.

Her only choice is to take him back inside. The mice have moved to a foreign country, learned the language, and now the place that was once home is strange, full of potential peril. She will have to adjust. Back in the living room, she tips the bucket on its side. The mouse rushes underneath the couch.

As though to test her resolve, another mouse is quivering beneath the eye of the bathtub drain that night. She frees her in the walk-in closet, then sets out finger dishes of water and feta crumbles for her miniature guests. The mice emerge in packs. Tucked into the top bunk, gently rubbing her stomach, she listens to the cabin rustling. Knowing that the mice are responsible for the noise doesn't lessen her fear. Sometimes the unexpected happens, and you have to decide if it's a miracle or just the opposite.

To give the mice their space, she contemplates sleeping on an air mattress on the deck, but that would mean contending with the slugs, who might be tempted to lay a sticky silver trail across her pillow in the middle of the night. Slugs do not interest her; though gastropods, they are all body and no shell. She moves her meals from the table to the couch, where she can keep her feet in plain sight. After eating, she naps. Then she combs the beach for treasures. Her collection of shells has taken over the kitchen counter: the clamshells come in two varieties like potato chips: traditional or ridged. Mussels are shaped like thumbs and so intensely green they appear black. The spiraled snails are as small as a baby's pupils, and she can find them only by sitting on a log and studying the sand in the small area between her feet. The big snail shells are thick with calcification and brilliant white and soft from being dragged back and forth across the sand. Faded browns and grays pattern Chinaman hats, and the warty exteriors of oysters hide their iridescent insides. She wonders whether Dale would object to her collecting shells on the grounds that she is appropriating creatures' homes for her own selfish pleasure. Probably. She arranges them in pleasing designs.

One night as she eats—her plate of steak, steamed asparagus, and dirty potatoes balanced on her stomach, her feet propped up on the armrest of the sofa, her sparkling water on the floor—the baby kicks. This is impossible. Her mind must be playing tricks on her. At this stage, the heartbeat is barely visible, the baby just a four-inch wisp of cells, buds of baby teeth, soft nails. And yet she is sure. She puts her plate on the ground and cradles her stomach, even though it is still mostly flat, and waits for the baby to move again. Now there is no denying the something inside of her, the thing that kicks, the baby, the baby that she and Dale have made. Another tiny ripple. She begins to cry. In the kitchen, the mice are scrambling, scratching, gnawing. They are sampling everything, wasteful little creatures. They nibble a corner of a granola bar before they change their minds and break into a box of cereal for a flake or two.

Deirdre's clothes are strewn across the floor along with piles of books and magazines, glasses choked with cherry pits and orange rinds and shriveled slices of lime and cucumber. Dale would be appalled. The baby is quiet now, gone, turned back into a motionless thing sleeping inside of her. What do you think of mice, little one? She pushes herself up from the couch, filled with resolve to tidy up, but just then three mice mosey around the corner and stop in the middle of the living room, sitting back on their hind legs and waving their pointy noses in the air like orchestra conductors. That night Deirdre sleeps on the couch, shifting uncomfortably and dreaming of small things: *Our cupboards are emptying,* they tell her. *Soon they will be bare.*

The next morning, Deirdre goes into the bathroom off the master bedroom. Here, the light is good, and there is a full-length mirror on the back of the door. She looks like she has eaten a large meal, but otherwise nothing is different. She probes her stomach with her fingers, trying to find the small thing, but it seems to have folded itself up and disappeared into a tight nook.

There is another mouse in the bathtub, a gray one, just like the one trapped earlier in the week, trying to climb the slippery walls. She wonders whether mice have suicidal impulses. She imagines this one darting along the edge, gathering speed, then veering into nothingness, its tiny paws still moving.

"I put water out for you," she scolds. "Why didn't you drink it?"

The phone rings. When the answering machine clicks on, Dale clears his throat. "Deirdre, are you there?" He pauses. "Uh, well, I just wanted to tell you that the crystal cat burned a hole in the wooden table next to the window. I guess she's like a magnifying glass. I smelled something burning and thought I'd left the stove on. Well . . . I feel dumb talking into the answering machine. It would be easier telling you this in person. Anyway, when I came back, I saw smoke curling up from the table. That cat really heats up. I burned my thumb. Can you imagine what would have happened if we'd both been away?"

Our apartment would have burned down, Deirdre thinks. Or, like the cabin, it might have been infested with mice. She has an irrational urge to pick up the phone and yell: "Things happen, Dale. They just happen."

He pauses again, his breath raspy and audible. "Well, okay, then. Good-bye."

She walks. It is easier to leave the cabin to the mice, and the upper island is crisscrossed with trails to explore. She laces on her hiking boots, packs herself a lunch—two bologna sandwiches, slices of cheese, crackers, orange soda, apples. Beef jerky for a snack. A liter of water. The lower half of the island was cleared fifty years ago, but the upper island is thick with Douglas-fir, cedars, spruce, and other trees she doesn't know. Halfway up the big hill, the pavement ends, and the road turns first to gravel and then to dirt. She passes the hulking metal water tanks where the water that is piped from the first lake is purified, the small electric station, the road to the old dump. At Horseshoe Lake, she sits on the steps of a small cabin that was built by loggers, the island's early inhabitants. She spots something floating in the middle of the lake and moves down to the small dock. It's a canoe. "Hello," she calls out, because it's just far enough away that she can't see it clearly. "Is someone out there?" Something rustles, and she feels a tinge of fear, but a deer steps out of the trees and gracefully lowers its head to drink. She wonders where the boat will stop.

The next day, she hikes all the way to Spencer, the second lake, where the island's oldest families keep their rafts for picnicking and fishing. Her family's sank several years ago. She passes the one-room schoolhouse. "In 1934," it says in spidery cursive on the old chalkboard, "the last year the school was in use, Miss Jean Davidson was the teacher. Five children were enrolled: two second graders, one third grader, a fifth grader and a ninth grader." This has been posted for the past twenty years, since Deirdre was a girl, and yet every year, she stops to admire the wood-burning stove, the old-fashioned desks connected to each other like beads on a string, the upper- and lowercase alphabet stenciled in cursive around three sides of the room. Standing against the blackboard, careful not to touch the writing, she thinks about how she first met Dale—they like to joke it was at a bowling league for left-handed singles, but really it was just a bowling club. For a nanosecond, bowling was hip, and they were hip, Deirdre in her platform Pradas that she'd reluctantly exchange for clumsy bowling shoes, and Dale in his orange corduroys, his wool newsie hat. They'd both grown up in Seattle, gone away, returned. They knew the same dive bars, the crumpet shop in the market, the deli where the owner cured his own meat. They both rented top-floor apartments in Victorians, invested in the notion they could walk away whenever opportunity called. After a while, Dale came to the alley with wonderful snacks: wild rice and hazelnut salad, miniature chèvre tarts, stuffed grape leaves, chunks of fresh lamb skewered on rosemary branches and grilled over mesquite. Back then, he cooked anything.

She glances around the schoolhouse again. How can it remain exactly the same year after year? It doesn't seem right. There is a thick piece of chalk in the tin cup on the teacher's desk, and in a corner of the board, she writes in a ghost hand, "I was here."

On the third day, she does something she's never done before. She heads for the wooden bathtub house. Walking up the big hill is easier, or perhaps she's grown more patient with the pace of walking. A man in a truck passes and shouts, does she want a ride, but she smiles and waves him forward. He's only the second person she's seen all week. There may be other people on the island, people who are hiding out as she is, or people who just seem to be hiding but are actually going about their quiet routines. She passes the first lake and the pasture where the lonely black horse grazes. She passes the big organic garden where she has, in years past, snuck in and stolen raspberries. She passes the road to the summit. When she was a teenager, it was a great adventure to try to ride up there in the dark on motorbikes. Finally, she reaches the turnoff to the wooden bathtub house. Perhaps she visited as a child, or perhaps she has just heard stories about the place. The road is deeply rutted, and when she isn't paying attention, mud squishes over the toes of her boots. Trees stand at strange angles, and she sees an astonishing sight—six saplings, almost evenly placed, growing out of the trunk of a toppled-over tree. She's not thinking about anything. She's not thinking about Dale, or the problems of their relationship, or the mouse in the bathtub, or whether the wooden bathtub will be teeming with mice. No, she is deeply engrossed in the rutted road and the beautiful mess of the forest, where things are rotting and growing in equal numbers and moss stubbles everything in shades of green, including some she has never noticed before.

The road turns, and she spots the cabin through the trees, but when she draws closer, nothing is there, except for a small pond guarded by cattails. Deirdre trips. It's a terrible feeling, falling forward as the body automatically recalibrates, shifting weight backward and trying to outfinesse the insistent grip of momentum and gravity. But it's too late. She lands heavily. She doesn't even get her hands out in time to break the fall. She lies still for a few moments before gently touching her stomach.

The mouse is dead. His once wiry and sleek body is lumpy and swollen now, and his face looks bruised and tormented. He has been dead for days, but now that he is rotting, Deirdre can no longer peer down at him in the bathtub's bottom and pretend he is dreaming of nuts and seeds and small dark places and stuffing. The smell makes her vomit. Her hip has a purple bruise. The small thing—her baby—is holding itself very still right now. She calls Dale. "I'm pregnant," she blurts out.

He is silent for a moment. "Are you leaving me?"

"But maybe not."

"I don't understand."

"I fell."

"What are you telling me?" he demands.

She feels sorry for herself. She is so irresponsible. Is it really possible to stop loving someone for no good reason? "I wasn't paying attention."

"Why didn't you tell me?"

"I killed another mouse," she says.

"What?"

"I left it in the bathtub," she says. "I didn't rescue it."

"Why didn't you tell me you were pregnant?"

"I don't know," she says. "But you're not listening to me. I let the mouse die. I didn't do anything."

He is silent for a moment, though Deirdre can hear his anger and frustration drawing the phone line taut. How can you know someone so well, and also know so little? "Never mind," he says. "What matters right now is whether the baby is okay. Are you bleeding?"

"No," she says, "there's no blood."

She listens as Dale tells her the arrangements he'll make to bring her back to Seattle. "I'll call back in five minutes," he says, and she thanks him and adds that she is sorry. On the railing of the deck, there is the cup, there is the small creature curled in the bottom. She flings the dead mouse into the darkness and flies with him, not knowing where her toss will take her, or whether she is still light enough to touch down softly, or how she'll feel when she finishes turning into something new.

AWESOME

When I first hitched my pony to Burt's treat truck, I assumed that he was just like the other guys I'd been dating, guys who were still finding themselves: treat truck employee by day, aspiring rock star by night, or something along those lines. Under his white apron, Burt wore skinny jeans, Star Wars and Battlestar Galactica T-shirts, and clunky boots, and he was never without a funny old-man hat. He'd bought the truck with money he earned putting a perfect sear on New York strip and creaming spinach during the week and running an underground supper club out of his Williamsburg loft on the weekends, and he dreamed of someday managing a whole fleet of trucks, each one with a different menu, sensibility, and soundtrack.

On our fourth date, Burt told me he wanted to take me someplace special.

"Where?" I said, guessing he meant the old wooden roller coaster out at Coney Island or a dive bar in Red Hook.

Then he named a French restaurant I'd read about in the *Times*.

"No way," I said.

"I've been saving up for months," he said. "This is French, but without the sauciness. The chef is foaming everything. Picture it: Beet foam! Wasabi foam! Turkish coffee foam! And then he's got all these cool tricks he does with liquid nitrogen."

Burt's enthusiasm was contagious. "Are you serious?" I asked, referring to both the food and the invitation. At this point, we hadn't even slept together. Our dates culminated in increasingly long sessions of stoop kissing that left my legs the consistency of firm Jell-O. (Burt believed that homemade gelatin in exotic flavors had great market potential.) But I didn't invite Burt up to my apartment, and he didn't press for an invitation. His hesitation seemed to match my own. We had no shared context, since we'd met in the cookbook section of the Strand, where we were both hunting for Julia Child's bible on French cooking. He was buying a copy as a wedding present for his best friend, and I was embarking on self-improvement in the most predictable way possible. I was doing a lot of self-renovation in those days, trying to turn myself into a person with spacious, light-filled interiors.

"As serious as you want me to be," Burt said.

"What?" I felt my face turning red.

Burt's eyes locked on mine. "I just mean I like you."

"I like you too." Even though I'd said these words—and more serious ones—to half a dozen guys whom I probably liked less than Burt, they sounded hollow, other things I didn't care to hear rattling around inside of them. Once you gave voice to your feelings, things could get so complicated.

Burt laughed. "You're a conundrum, Sylvie. Sylvie-who-has-fun-until-the-end-of-the-evening-and-then-disappears."

"I don't know about that," I said, already taking a step back, losing my balance for just a second because of the doormat.

Burt sighed. "It'll be my treat, by the way."

"No," I said. "I couldn't let you do that."

"Well, we'll see," he said before taking his own step backwards. He held my hand until too much distance opened between us. Then, after smiling hopefully, he turned and walked away. This never happened. Usually I took the stairs by two. Usually I arranged things so that I was the one who left first.

Before Burt, I had only dated guys who were not Lance. It's hard to explain what Lance had meant to me. There was the Lance before we dated, the Lance who'd been my doctor when I was a teenager, whom I'd liked because he was the rare adult who listened, who seemed to find me worthy of regular conversations and not the kind of watered-down attention that adults manufacture for younger people. Then there was the Lance who knew me as a young woman, who just happened to be passing through wherever I was living and sent me tickets and took me places and introduced me to experiences: Lebanese food, canyoneering, left-wing magazines, salsa and merengue, the man with whom I had long philosophical conversations, the man who seemed to want to know me, who could appreciate my wanderlust, who treated me as his equal and was, according to my mother, my hometown's most eligible bachelor. In my early twenties, I didn't see myself as grown up and couldn't imagine competing with real women (whatever that meant) for the attention of a man they wanted. This was why for many years I didn't think he could like me, even though the tension was palpable, even though I thought I'd made my feelings clear by sending him flirtatious postcards that I addressed to my "Western Muse" and making him heartbreakingly silly things, like a ceramic jar that I filled with fortune cookies: "If you look in the right places, you can find some good offerings." Hint. Hint. "Soon life will become more interesting."

Lance disappeared for several years after Laurie died. Actually, I was the one who vanished. I'd had a chance and blown it. After that weekend in Santa Fe, I fantasized about him often—crude, funny scenes of seduction that make me cringe now—while I was with other men. I knew this was a bad idea, but I couldn't seem to stop myself.

The Lance while we were dating was someone else. At first, it was better than I had ever imagined. We continued our custom of meeting in different places every couple of weeks, and we went on amazing, exotic trips—to Spain, Hawaii, and even Zanzibar, flying first class and staying in the kind of hotels I'd only glimpsed in travel magazines. There was always a moment, when a driver holding a sign that read "Mr. and Mrs. Peters" in clear block letters greeted us or a bellhop opened the doors of a hired car and welcomed us to a boutique hotel, when I would see or imagine seeing these men doing a double-take, looking from Lance to me and back to Lance, and the hair on my arms stood up. I thought marrying Lance would be a continuation of these adventures, only no one would question my appearance with a man visibly older than me, and it wouldn't give me pause either. When we weren't traveling, we would live in a modern house filled with beautiful things (because Lance already possessed many beautiful objects) and books, and we would have two children, even though Lance doubted he wanted even one, and we would respect each other's independence, and blah blah blah.

Lance pointed to a locked wooden chest in the middle of his living room. "Do you know what's in there?"

This was my first visit to his house as his girlfriend instead of his friend.

"A dead body," I joked.

"No, though close," he said. "It's your dowry."

"What?"

"I'm joking, but everything in here is for you." He opened the chest and began sifting through its contents, probing the shape of paper bags buttery-soft from age, while I perched on the edge of the sofa, feigning nothing more than a mild interest in what was inside.

"Ah," he said, peering into a small white box, "I remember this. It's from my favorite jewelry store in Denver."

At the time, it seemed like the most romantic thing in the world. He'd loved me for longer than I could have imagined, and he had the goods to prove it. During his many travels, sometimes with other women, sometimes solo, he'd always picked up a little something for me. Yes, he laughed, he occasionally lied and told these women—whose names I'd just learned from the disconcerting shrine of framed photos of girlfriends past on a bookshelf—that he was buying the batik for his mother or the pistachio green silk jacket for his sister, but what did it matter? "You've been on my mind for a long time."

"Are you going to give me something?" I asked playfully, gravitating forward, toward both Lance and the open chest.

"No," he said, sitting back on his heels.

"But . . ." I was suddenly disgusted and frightened by the amount of greed I felt. "They're for me."

"Yes, but they're mine," he answered. "They remind me of the feeling I had for you."

"But we're together now."

"Right," he said. "Now I have you, but when I bought these things I didn't, and I didn't know whether I would ever have you." He walked on his knees toward me. He pressed his face into my pubic bone. "You don't know what it was like," he said in a muffled voice that I barely recognized, "not knowing whether this would ever work out."

On the night of the big French dinner, the night that was at once the beginning and nearly the end of us, I recognized Burt on the Fourteenth Street subway platform by his brown fedora. From a distance, with a book pressed close to his face, he was not the man of my dreams, or even, for that matter, a man I was sure I wanted to have dinner with. I'd also started to wonder about the timing of his invitation. To get Saturday night, Burt must have made the reservation months ago with someone else in mind. I was, I'd been telling myself, a replace-a-date.

For a moment, I considered rushing back up the stairs, through the turnstile, and out onto the crowded sidewalks. No one would be able tell how scared and cruel I was, and over time, the decision would fade from my memory as well. But then Burt folded his book around his finger and glanced at his watch, and I found myself moving as though walking a tightrope toward him.

"Hey," I said. In my heels, I could kiss him without standing on my tiptoes. I hadn't considered this when I was getting dressed. Was this a mistake? Was I too tall? These shoes dated back to the Lance era.

"Hey, you," Burt said. "You clean up nice."

"So do you," I said shyly.

Up close, it was easier to remember Burt's charms. He was wearing a pinstripe suit with a vest and pointy black cowboy boots. His brown hair was slicked back except where it curled impishly at his temples. He looked like a lion tamer or an old-fashioned sheriff. Linking his arm through mine, he drew me closer.

"And how did you spend the day, my pretty?" This was a real question since we saw each other just once a week.

"I ran across the Brooklyn Bridge."

"Mon dieu." He touched his cheek to mine, a more intimate gesture than a kiss. "How far is that?"

"Just five."

"Five miles?" he gasped in mock surprise.

He was being very silly.

"And I thought I had it rough," he continued.

"Was it a good day at Tastiness in a Truck?" I knew enough about Burt's routine to know he parked near Prospect Park on Saturdays.

"Women swooning over my pork belly sandwiches."

I touched his bicep lightly. "That sounds very trying."

"Man, it was. I'm gonna have to start stocking smelling salts."

"Can I ask you . . ." But I was interrupted by the keening of the uptown express. Finding out whether he'd planned to bring another woman to dinner suddenly seemed like a sure way to make the evening mournful. I pressed my fingernails into my palm to keep things in perspective.

"What's that?" he asked when the noise had passed.

"You smell nice." This was a small joke between us—one of the few we shared. On our first date he'd come straight from work reeking of garlic and then spent the whole evening apologizing. He did smell good, some tasty combination of mint and rosemary.

He sniffed my neck. "What a coincidence! You smell nice, and I smell nice . . ."

"I was at the Strand, and you were at the Strand . . ."

He playfully slugged me. "I was breathing air, and you were breathing air, and we realized we were both breathing the same air . . ."

"And it was meant to be." I raised one eyebrow.

"Don't do that."

"What?" I did it again.

"When you do that . . ." He growled, and I blushed.

By the time we reached the restaurant, we had settled into a comfortable banter, but my self-consciousness returned as soon as I had shrugged off my jacket and stood in my tight white and black sweater and short black skirt. These presents from Lance had been interred in garment bags since we broke up. They had cost more than a month's rent. I told myself I didn't wear them not because they brought back painful memories, but because they reminded me of how willing I'd been to change who I was. Or so I thought.

"Wow," Burt said, a smile playing on his lips. "Wow," he repeated. "You look really, really good."

I couldn't think of anything to say.

"Shall I take that?" the hostess asked.

"Umm." Since I wasn't carrying a purse, I'd stowed my wallet, lipstick, and mints in the pocket of my coat. "Is it okay if I keep it?"

"As you like," the hostess said.

Burt raised his arm to signal my place in the procession toward our table. I knew the order. I knew that Burt would, if he were a certain kind of man, place his hand on the small of my back and steer me toward the table, but he didn't. Instead, he whistled a watery tune that was so quiet and subtle it could have almost passed for breathing.

The restaurant was very beige: beige walls, beige carpet, beige chairs, beige people. The tablecloths were off-white. Glass vases of purple and fuchsia as tall as trees sprung up in the middle of the room. The art looked famous. The people looked famous or, if not famous, important or wealthy. It was the kind of place Lance would have chosen, the kind of place where I would have sat on the edge of my seat, my body too charged to relax. It was oddly exhilarating to feel out of place. And also: wearying. Once, confronted with a menu with no prices at a three-star restaurant, I got so nauseated I told Lance I needed to return to the hotel. But he wouldn't hear of it. He and the maître d' had a whispered conversation, and then the maître d' took my arm, guiding me to a room with a small bed, where he covered me with a blanket. Moments later, he returned carrying two glasses, one filled with milk, the other with anise-flavored fizzy water. "Drink, sleep," he told me, "Soon you ready for delicious." When I returned to the table an hour later, Lance was beaming. "Baby, you've risen from the dead." He'd toured the kitchen, had a glass of wine with the chef, and ordered us a special tasting menu. "Are you up for it?" he asked. I said I was, and it was true. We ate for five hours that night, one of the best meals of my life.

Now I found myself trying to recall whether Burt had taken off his hat, but I didn't dare look back at him.

"Here we are," the hostess said.

Cramped and with a view straight into the swinging door of the kitchen, the table was the least desirable in the room. Lance would have immediately raised a stink, but Burt just smiled. "Cool," he said rubbing his hands together. "This looks great."

"It's cozy," I said.

"It's perfect," he said, removing his hat now and settling it on the edge of the table, where it looked as out of place as a small roosting bird.

"I think you should put your hat under the table." I felt my nose scrunch up.

"Don't let me forget it," he said, winking at me. He knocked a bread plate off the table. My jaw tightened.

"It's a flying saucer," Burt said, leaning over and picking it up. "Get it?"

I counterfeited a smile and twisted my heavy linen napkin around my finger. To Burt, it probably looked like a small animal ferreting around in my lap.

When the waiter came to explain the menu, I was sure he detected that this was a special occasion for us, though not in a good way, more like kids playing dress-up, kids wobbling around in their parents' shoes and holding up their parents' pants. We would be treated poorly, I imagined; the dinner Burt had been looking forward to would be ruined; or I would singlehandedly spoil everything by continuing to be as stiff and stupid as a plastic Barbie doll.

"Do you have any questions?" the waiter asked.

If it had been me, I would have said, "No, nononono," not wanting to impose on the waiter, eager to escape his sham solicitous manner. But not Burt. He leaned forward, tilted his head up, his eyes as eager as a child's glimpsing a soft-serve ice cream machine, and wondered about preparations and ideal wine pairings. He asked whether the tasting menu was the way to go. He inquired about the provenance of the oysters and the marinade on the hamachi. "A reduction of grapefruit juice frozen in liquid nitrogen?" Burt gasped, and the waiter seemed to blush.

"And which do you prefer," Burt pressed on, "the turbot or the skate?"

The waiter was biting his words, swallowing whole syllables—*escargot* sounded like *cargo*, *poisson* like *puss*—and simultaneously fidgeting, though very, very subtly. I thought I could see his mouth twitching and his toes wiggling in his shoes when Burt added, "This dinner is a very big deal. I've been looking forward to it for months. I was going to bring my father, but then I had the good luck to meet Sylvie."

Right then, I felt such a complicated mixture of emotions: relief that I had not been Burt's second choice and exasperation with myself for always tending to believe the worst and disbelief as I listened to Burt describe our last date, when we'd taken the train up the Hudson and spent the day picking apples: "A crisp fall day, perfect really, except that we picked more apples than we could carry."

It wouldn't have surprised me if he'd produced a jar of apple butter and presented it to the waiter. I wanted to disappear into the bathroom and sit on the toilet with my head between my knees, maybe even do a quick handstand, anything to shake the feeling of embarrassment.

"This deserves some champagne," the waiter said. I think he even winked, as cheesy as that sounds. "It's on me."

The waiter was smiling without a trace of pity. I looked at Burt, his surprise and pleasure so real, his eyes were sparkling. I used to believe this only happened in books, but I swear I could see it.

"*That* would be awesome," Burt said.

I smiled. It was a totally involuntary reflex, but I couldn't help myself. I picked up an empty wineglass. It was childish, and maybe unlucky or impolite, to toast without something in your glass. "To an awesome beginning," I found myself saying, even though I hated the word *awesome*. It was one of those grand words that had been ruined by people who didn't know its original meaning, who thought it merely meant *cool,* but suddenly I didn't care.

"To many more adventures," Burt said, looking me directly in the eyes while I did my best to hold his gaze.

After Lance and I had been dating for six months or so, when we started talking on the phone regularly, our conversations were seeded with uncomfortable silences. I would tell him about the details of my day—a book on the origins of haiku that I was editing or a funny exchange with my boss about his most recent disastrous date—and he wouldn't say anything. Afterward I would pace, clenching the phone like a small, rather useless weapon, wondering whether I should call him back. Whenever I did, when I asked, "Is everything okay?" or "Are you okay?" he would parrot back, "Are you okay, Sylvie?" Laugh. "I'm just fine."

Lance also started coming to New York more often. When we were together, we shrugged off the awkwardness, found our groove. He'd book a fancy hotel, a new one each time, and I'd pack my duffel bag and take the subway from Fort Greene to midtown and spend the weekend pretending to be a tourist. We'd roam Central Park, take in a singer-songwriter not yet quite famous, see a documentary about one small example of how shitty the world was, and discuss it for hours afterward. When we were together we were mostly good.

Lance liked to shop. We'd wander into stores along Madison or Fifth Avenue, and Lance would pick out clothes for me to try on. He liked to sit on the slightly perfumed chairs outside the dressing room and evaluate each outfit.

The first time, I tried to hide in the dressing room. In the mirror, I looked like a child pretending to be a grown-up, my head stuck on a body that I didn't recognize, that somehow seemed too womanly now that it was in a fitted sweater, trousers that nipped my waist. This kind of shopping was too intimate. I planned to yell through the slats that nothing worked, but the door whipped open, and there was Lance, his face eager and expectant, and the saleslady pronouncing: "She looks fabulous. These clothes, they're meant for a body like hers."

"She does look beautiful," Lance said, squinting, appraising my body without looking at me, "but I think she needs some heels."

"I'm too tall. I don't do heels," I protested, but no one was listening. Lance wandered off with the saleslady and her smiling hips. When she said something, he leaned toward her conspiratorially, and they both laughed, and I found myself feeling pleased and jealous, delighted and wounded. I bit my cheek.

I was relieved when Lance didn't buy me anything that day. I had a vague idea how much our whole affair was costing him, and it was starting to make me feel nervous. Three months later, he emerged from his walk-in closet carrying a tower of five boxes festooned with purple ribbons. "What is this?" I might have squealed. I might have even jumped up and down on the bed, like a little girl being introduced to a new pony or kitten.

"Happy New Year, baby," Lance said, arranging the boxes around me on the bed before choosing one and shaking it. "Hmmm, not this one." He shook another. "Not this one, either. Maybe this one."

The boxes exhaled the scent of luxury as I eased them open. At the sight of the black sweater, I might have shrieked again and again, "I can't believe it."

I'm sure I gave Lance a passionate kiss. He liked a certain kind of passion, which is why he relished staying in hotels so much. All those mirrors. And then I stripped off my clothes and began trying on my presents, piece by piece, walking an imaginary runway, while he lay propped up on pillows in bed, calling out compliments.

I returned to the restaurant to fetch Burt's hat, where he'd forgotten it under the table. "That one's a cutie-pie," the waiter said, dropping the French and speaking Brooklyn. "He's a real keeper."

I put on Burt's funny hat and tipped it in his direction.

I wanted to sleep with Burt that night. Though I don't believe there's a single moment when you know you've finally found the right person—I mean, come on, I'd felt that way with Lance when I was surrounded by all the beautiful clothes he'd bought—me! with those gorgeous expensive clothes!—I still sometimes catch myself thinking that, of course, something changed when Burt said, "Awesome!" As we rode toward Fourteenth Street, where he would go east and I would head downtown, Burt said, "How 'bout coming back to my place for a nightcap?"

I laughed. "Let me change into my smoking jacket."

"And I'll slip into something more comfortable."

Burt walked his hand around my shoulder, and I relaxed into his embrace, even though I usually cringed at public shows of affection, especially in the fluorescent-lit subway car, where it was impossible to fade into the background. We seemed to fit together like a ball in a socket.

"So?" He doodled on my shoulder.

"Write something," I said. "See if I can decipher it."

I pushed up my sleeve, closed my eyes. His fingers felt like an eraser, instead of the ticklish tip of a pen or pencil. "All work and no play make Jack a very dull boy," I guessed wildly.

"Close. Not."

"Write it again."

"You have to wait for me to finish," he said.

"Okay." I moistened my lips, the taste of the chocolate petit fours the waiter had brought as a gift lingering. "Peter Piper picked a peck of pickled peppers . . ."

"No," he said, "but you do have a very nimble tongue."

"Indeed," I said, "if Peter Piper picked a peck of pickled peppers, how many pickled peppers did Peter Piper pick?"

Burt kissed me.

"No distractions," I said.

He traced something else. "Red Rover."

"Good," he said. "Two words. You're getting warmer." He wrote them again.

"Calf groper?" I said. " 'If I warned you once, I warned you a million times: don't grope the young livestock.' "

He snickered. "Your unconscious is very revealing, my sweet."

I cracked open an eye. Burt was grinning.

"Come over," he said.

"Come over?" I said.

"Like come over tonight," he said. "Really."

"I can't." This was my default response.

"What?" he said.

"I just can't," I said. "Okay?"

I expected him to wheedle me, coax me, keep asking and even begging me, jokingly of course, to spend the night with him. It was all a dance. That's what worked with me. A big scene. I'd rush off the subway, rush back on. With enough drama, I didn't have to take responsibility. All I had to do was eventually give in. He didn't say anything. At the very least, I thought he would say, "Okay."

But Burt—Burt, Bertie, Hubert, Hue—he left. Walked right away.

By the time I got back to my apartment, I was in a state. I rushed into my room—which my roommates, two nice men with whom I had a cozy domestic situation, had helped me paint the most peaceful shade of green—and rifled through my closet until I found the things I needed: a silk jacket with a spray of embroidered flowers across the back. A blue shirt that fit perfectly through the bust. Sexy thigh-high boots. A gorgeous military-inspired wool suit. I muscled open the window. I planned to heave this and all the other fucking things that Lance had given me out of the window with Laurie, or her ghost, rooting me on: "You go, Sylvie!"

She would have approved. When she needed to, she could pull out the grand gesture. Once, as the last hour before she would hear the results of some test dawdled by, she sat on the lumpy couch in our cramped walk-up with a big, shiny box of chocolates on her lap. She bit off the bottoms, studied their centers. When she liked what she saw, she popped the whole thing into her mouth. When she didn't, she pitched it, half eaten, out the window.

"Life is too short for the fruits," she said.

Consider getting struck by a sweet on Bleecker.

As I stood there with cold air huffing through the window,

I decided that what I really needed to do was call Burt. "I'm so sorry," I cried when he picked up after an excruciating five rings. "I'm on my way over."

"It's too late, Sylvia," he said. "Just go to bed."

"But I want to come over," I said. "Really and truly."

"Not tonight," he said, hanging up and leaving me with the empty hum of a broken connection.

I climbed into bed, the window still open, the cold air rushing in, the clothes piled carelessly on the floor. In another time, in another place, they would have been the punctuation—the exclamation points, the sexy question marks, the unbearably slow commas—of a night of frenzied passion. Evidence of a striptease motivated mostly by teasing instead of a desire to lay anything of importance bare.

Lance had been about the grand gesture, the exotic trips and the sun setting over a dhow in the East Indian Ocean, the impulsive ideas (to drive on down to the all-night chapel in Vegas and just do it, baby), the surprise visits, the folksingers sent to my doorstep to serenade me, the locked treasure chest in his living room.

But, of course, I had loved the grand gesture just as much as he had. I'd believed in the great heroic possibility of his unwavering love. When it turned out the most eligible bachelor did have a girlfriend or girlfriends, which was why we always slept in separate beds, I believed him when he told me he couldn't marry any of these other women until he'd seen what it was like to be with me.

Tonight, I finally made a choice: I'd just go to bed. Period. I wouldn't wind up standing on the fire escape in my underwear, surveying the abstract arrangement of jackets and skirts, blouses, and trousers on the asphalt below.

Someday I would understand that the day I begged and wheedled and pleaded with Lance to *please, pretty pretty please, baby, open the fucking trunk* was the beginning of the end of our relationship.

It took a good thirty minutes to empty the chest. Another thirty for me to peek in boutique bags, mine objects from paper confetti, cut through packing tape and candy-striped twine, demummify fragile goods swaddled in butcher paper, bubble wrap, foreign newspapers, and, in one case, a man's stained undershirt.

In the end, I had a whole bunch of stuff that I didn't want. I'd pillaged a burial site that didn't belong to me. A teeny-tiny pink tie-dyed bikini sent me into hysterical laughter.

"You don't like it?" Lance asked.

"It's just not me," I said.

"Really," he said. "I thought it was you."

Months later, I discovered a lopsided list that Lance had written in grade-school cursive: *Sylvie—Pros and Cons.* "I'm sorry," he said as I cried. "I didn't mean for you to see it all spelled out. But you're not the woman who I loved."

Someday Burt and I would get married. But in the meantime there was just tomorrow, when I would call Burt and thank him for the incredible dinner and also apologize. And the next night and the night after that and every night for several weeks. It would seem like a long, agonizing time before he agreed to go out with me again. When he said, "I don't know about you," my only choice would be to take the risk of showing him that he did know about me just as I knew about him.

Acknowledgments

Thank you to Malena Watrous, Tom McNeely, Pamela Painter, Kate Wheeler, Paige Reynolds, and Shawn Maurer for reading these stories along the way; Geoff Demers for providing shelter and great adventures in New Mexico while I finished this collection; and my family, Scott Reents and Caitlin Van Dusen, their sons, Sebastian and Ivan, and Sue and Henry Reents for their enduring love and joy. I am grateful for the support of the Holy Cross English department, the Stegner Program at Stanford University, especially John L'Heureux, Tobias Wolff, and Elizabeth Tallent, the Bread Loaf Writers Conference, Michael Koch, editor of *Epoch,* and Laura Furman, editor of *The PEN/O. Henry Prize Stories.* Finally, I am happily indebted to my terrific editor, Alexis Washam, the incomparable Emily Forland, whose unshakeable optimism, intelligence, and kindness has kept me going for many years, and Deb Jane Addis, best sister-friend and most generous reader.

About the Author

Born and raised in Boise, Idaho, STEPHANIE REENTS has lived in a shared flat in Oxford, England, a tiny studio on the wrong side of the tracks in Idaho Falls, a fifth-floor walk-up in Manhattan's West Village, an adobe near the Sonora desert, a garden apartment in the Upper Haight of San Francisco, and the old Hamilton Watch Factory building in Lancaster, Pennsylvania. Her fiction has been included in *The PEN/O. Henry Prize Stories,* noted in *Best American Short Stories,* and has appeared in numerous journals. She teaches in the English department at College of the Holy Cross and lives in Providence, Rhode Island.

About the Author